D0056285

ALEX MORGAN

Simon & Schuster Books for Young Readers
New York   London   Toronto   Sydney   New Delhi

SIMON & SCHUSTER BOOKS FOR YOUNG READERS

An imprint of Simon & Schuster Children's Publishing Division

1230 Avenue of the Americas, New York, New York 10020

This book is a work of fiction. Any references to historical events, real people, or real places are used fictitiously. Other names, characters, places, and events are products of the author's imagination, and any resemblance to actual events or places or persons, living or dead, is entirely coincidental.

SIMON & SCHUSTER BOOKS FOR YOUNG READERS

is a trademark of Simon & Schuster, Inc.

For information about special discounts for bulk purchases, please contact Simon & Schuster Special Sales at 1-866-506-1949 or business@simonandschuster.com.

The Simon & Schuster Speakers Bureau can bring authors to your live event. For more information or to book an event, contact the Simon & Schuster Speakers Bureau at 1-866-248-3049 or visit our website at www.simonspeakers.com.

Book design by Krista Vossen

The text for this book was set in Berling.

Manufactured in the United States of America

0218 FFG

First Edition

2 4 6 8 10 9 7 5 3 1

Library of Congress Cataloging-in-Publication Data

Names: Morgan, Alex (Alexandra Patricia), 1989- author.

Title: In the zone / Alex Morgan.

Description: First edition. | New York : Simon & Schuster Books for Young Readers, [2018] | Series: The Kicks | Summary: Devin, a seventh-grader and co-captain of the soccer team, is worried that her friends' issues will keep them from being "in the zone" while playing.

Identifiers: LCCN 2017006501| ISBN 9781481481533 (hardcover) | ISBN 9781481481557 (ebook)

Subjects: | CYAC: Soccer—Fiction. | Teamwork (Sports)—Fiction. | Self-confidence—Fiction. | Friendship—Fiction. | Middle schools—Fiction. | Schools—Fiction.

Classification: LCC PZ7.M818 In 2018 | DDC [Fic]—dc23

LC record available at https://lccn.loc.gov/2017006501

CHAPTER ONE

"Devin!" a voice boomed out of the crowd.

I was warming up on the sidelines for the second game of the Kicks season, but I stopped my jumping jacks to scan the stands. I spotted my friend Steven waving a pair of white-and-blue pom-poms and doing a silly dance.

I started cracking up, laughing so hard that I doubled over with my hands around my waist.

"What's so funny?" my friend Jessi asked.

I couldn't stop giggling, but I pointed with my finger.

Jessi looked and broke out in a grin.

"Jessi!" Cody, sitting next to Steven, called as he waved and smiled at her. But he wasn't holding pom-poms in our team's colors like Steven was.

Steven had told me once that he was my biggest fan. Now I couldn't doubt him.

Steven, Cody, Jessi, and I all hung out together

sometimes. We were all in the seventh grade at Kentville Middle School. Jessi and I weren't allowed to date yet, but we really enjoyed spending time with the boys. Not only were they both soccer players and loved to talk about all things soccer, but Steven was super cute, and his smile was the best I'd ever seen. *Totally* adorable.

"Ugh!" Emma cried out in frustration. I tore my gaze away from Steven's antics to see what was wrong with my friend, the Kicks goalie.

"What's the matter?" I asked. Emma sat slumped on the grass, her knees bent and her hands tugging on her cleat laces.

"My laces broke!" she moaned. "Ever since that growth spurt I had in the winter, my feet are in between sizes. I can't find a pair of cleats that fit right. These are too loose. I tried pulling the laces really tight, and they ripped apart!"

I raised an eyebrow at that. The cleats' laces were made of this strong, stretchy fabric. Emma must have really been tugging hard to break them.

"Here, let me see if I can knot it," said Zoe, our resident fashionista and a whiz with all fabrics. She got onto the ground next to Emma and began fiddling with the laces.

"The timing is awful," Emma complained as Zoe worked. "The Rams are tough competition. I need to bring my A game. I can't have a problem with my cleats!"

"Don't worry, Emma," Frida reassured her. Not only was Frida a defender on the Kicks, but she was also an actor. She always got into character before a soccer game for motivation. "The goal is where the hidden treasure of Atlantis is buried. I am a mermaid warrior, sworn to defend it. I won't let anyone near you!"

Emma sighed. "I know. The Kicks have great defenders, but sometimes it's lonely at the goal. And when a ball gets through, it's like it's all my fault. All eyes are on me." She shook her head. "But I'm going to shake it all off and go out there and do my best!"

Emma was so positive all the time. Hearing her complain a minute earlier had been strange. I was glad to see the usual, upbeat Emma return. But it made me think about how much of a burden there was on the goalie. I was a forward, and I usually got pretty focused on always looking for scoring opportunities. While I had played goalie in practice, I'd never really given much thought to what it must be like to be a goalie all the time. Standing in front of the goal, all alone, waiting for that ball to come at you, knowing you alone had to stop it—that was a lot of responsibility. And Emma was so good at it.

"Here you go!" Zoe said as she stood up. "I did the best I can, but it might come undone."

"Hey, you don't think Emma's laces were sabotaged by the Rams, do you?" Jessi joked.

Frida rolled her eyes, Zoe sighed, and I shook my head, while Emma just laughed.

During the fall the Rams had played a lot of mean pranks on the Kicks to try to make us lose games. It hadn't

ALEX MORGAN

worked. We'd put a stop to what they were doing and had faced the Rams on the field and beat them fair and square. Jamie Quinn, the Rams captain, had been the ringleader. Because of that, I hadn't liked her very much. But I'd gotten to know her when we'd both been on the Griffons winter league team together. We were sort of friendly now.

In fact, she had even texted me before our last game against the Panthers.

GLNG, she'd written, which was short for "good luck next game." It might not have seemed like much, but for Jamie it was very warm and fuzzy.

"Nah, I'm just kidding," Jessi said. "Now that I know her, Jamie's not so bad."

"In fact, she's very good." Emma shuddered. "It's not fun to be in front of the goal when Jamie is taking a shot, let me tell you."

Emma was right. Jamie, and just about everyone else on the Rams, was a solid, strong player. The Kicks had faced them a few weeks before in a scrimmage and had lost.

Today was not a scrimmage. It was a game, and we wanted to win!

As Coach Flores called us over, I spotted my mom, dad, and little sister, Maisie, in the stands, holding a long GO KICKS! banner. I smiled as I sprinted over to Coach. Steven had a lot of competition to be my biggest fan.

"Listen up," Coach Flores said, a wide grin on her face. "You have all been killing it in practice. Your teamwork is on point, and your skills are improving every day, so go out there and do this!"

"Yes, Coach!" we all yelled back. The pregame energy was building, fueling us up.

Jamie was in the center spot as the Rams waited to receive the ball. Her long, blond hair was pulled into a ponytail, and she had her game face on. But she broke it just for a second to give me a wink. Then the ref blew his whistle, and the ball dropped.

Jamie got it and kicked it to one of her teammates, but before she could get the ball, Grace, an eighth grader and my co-captain on the Kicks, swooped in and stole it. She dribbled it down the field, and I tried to shake off the Rams defenders so I could be open for her pass. I faked moving to the left but started running to the right. Soon I was in the clear and had the goal in my sights.

"Devin!" Grace called out, and the ball came soaring to me.

I took the ball and raced toward the goal, my heart pounding. There's a feeling you get when the goal is in front of you and you have a clear shot. It's hard to describe, but the exhilaration is one thing that makes me love soccer. It's such a thrill.

Of course, it's more of a thrill when you make the goal, so I focused on that. The goalie was crouched and waiting, trying to figure out which direction I'd kick the ball.

I tilted to the right, making it look like I was going to kick the ball to the left, but at the last minute I pivoted, using my left foot to kick the ball as hard as I could into the goal. Time seemed to stop for a second as the ball flew from my foot and the Rams' goalie had to make a split-second decision: Go right or left?

The goalie lunged to her right, but my ball bounced into the back of the net on her other side.

The goalie and I gave shouts at the same time—hers of frustration, mine of celebration. I had made the first goal of the game!

"Way to go, Devin!" Hailey came over and high-fived me, and Jessi ran over to give me a quick hug. We were on our way.

That goal lit a fire under the Rams. A few minutes later Hailey had the ball and was dribbling it down the left side as two Rams charged for her. One of them stole it right out from under her and passed it to Jamie, who was waiting down the field, close to our goal.

Frida ran out to block Jamie.

"Who dares disturb the ancient treasure of Atlantis?" she bellowed.

Most players were so taken by surprise by Frida's antics that they fumbled the ball, but Jamie had nerves of steel. Plus, she had squared off against Frida before and knew what to expect.

Unfazed, Jamie zipped around Frida and took a shot. That was when I saw Emma. She was leaning over, fiddling with her shoelace and not paying attention to the field.

"Emma! Look alive!" Grace yelled, but it was too late. Emma looked up just in time to see the ball flying overhead.

The whistle blew. Score! We were tied 1–1.

"Sorry, guys!" Emma yelled. "This darn shoelace is driving me crazy!"

I sighed. Why had Emma's laces had to break today, of all days?

The Rams offense was playing an aggressive game. They weaved and dodged, and managed to shake off our defenders twice in a row. Frida's mermaid warrior was having a hard time keeping up with the attackers of ancient Atlantis.

Jamie had another shot lined up, but this time Emma was ready for her. She blocked the goal with a spectacular leap, catching it with the very tips of her fingers.

Each team was playing at its best. Every time the Kicks got control of the ball, one of the Rams managed to get it away from us. But we did the same to their attackers.

At halftime Coach gave us a pep talk. "The struggle is real," she said. "You've brought your best game today. So have the Rams. But I did notice some holes in their defense that you can exploit."

She gave us some tips on how to bypass the Rams' defense. She noticed that when one of our players got the ball, their defenders tended to group around that one person.

"If you get the ball, and they come charging at you,

try passing it if you can," Coach suggested. "Then the player you pass it to should have a clear path to the goal."

As we raced back onto the field, Steven still had the pom-poms out and was shaking them as he chanted: "Together we stand, together we fall, all for one, and one for all!"

Steven looked over at Cody, who was texting on his phone and not paying attention. Steven nudged him with his elbow. "One for all!" Cody halfheartedly echoed.

I laughed, but Jessi, who was next to me, rolled her eyes.

"It's so cute what Steven is doing for *you*," she said, sticking her lower lip out in a pout.

I could tell that she was mad that Cody wasn't giving the same effort for her. I felt bad, but I had to stay in the competitive zone and not worry about Jessi. We had a game to win!

Jessi got control of the ball at the start, and just as Coach had said, three Rams defenders came charging toward her. Jessi quickly passed it to Hailey before the Rams reached her. Hailey charged forward and took a clear shot at the goal when she got close enough. We were now 2–1.

The Rams' coach must have been giving similar tips, because their forwards started playing a passing game on the next play, quickly passing the ball from one to another. Our defenders didn't know where to run, and one of the

Rams managed to shoot the ball past Emma, tying up the game.

Both teams tightened up their defense in response to the goals, so we were back to square one, basically at a stalemate. One team would get control of the ball, but they'd never get far with it before the other team would take it. It was like we were playing a game of Hot Potato with a soccer ball!

With only a few seconds left in the game, it looked like we were going into penalty kicks to determine the winner. But then I heard the Rams yelling, "Go, go, go, go, go, go!"

Jamie had gotten control of the ball and was tearing down the field like she was on fire, with the goal in her sights. She easily outmaneuvered Giselle, one of our defenders, and had an open shot at the goal.

My heart froze. Was Emma ready?

I didn't have to worry. My friend stood alert in front of the goal, her eyes laser focused on Jamie. She was watching Jamie's every move to determine which way Jamie would kick the ball.

Jamie was bearing down on the goal, ready to take her shot. A powerful kick sent the ball flying into the right corner, high and tight.

Emma anticipated the shot and jumped to her left to intercept it. As she soared far into the air, she extended her leg, and her cleat, the one with the broken shoelace, went flying off. Her mouth opened wide in shock as it hit the frame of the goal and then ricocheted off. It came down on her head and bounced off. The ball whizzed past her and hit the back of the net, hard.

The whistle blew. Emma slumped on the grass, her hands covering her face. The game was over and the Rams had won!

CHAPTER TWO

I lined up with the rest of the Kicks to slap hands with the Rams, like teams do at the end of every game. I glanced back at Emma. She was sitting on the grass with her legs stretched out in front of her, not moving. I'd never seen her look so upset. She didn't even join the line with the rest of us.

After we finished congratulating the Rams, I jogged back to the goal and reached down to Emma. She reluctantly lifted up her hands, and I pulled her up.

"Oh my gosh, that was awful!" she said, and I saw that her eyes were tearing up a little bit. "My stupid shoe!"

Jessi, Zoe, and Frida joined us.

"It's okay, Emma," Jessi said. "It happens."

"The goalie's shoe flying off and smacking her in the head?" Emma asked. "When, exactly, does that happen?"

"Well, maybe *that* doesn't happen too often," Jessi

admitted. "But goalies miss goals all the time."

"But we're not supposed to. We have only one job," Emma countered. "And this was an important game. We'll never win the championship if we can't beat the Rams."

"The loss isn't just on you," I told her. "We could have been stronger. The offense, I mean. We could have scored more points."

"And I could have done a better job defending you," Frida added. "But those Rams—they're tough!"

Coach Flores blew her whistle and waved to us. I knew she wanted to go over the game with the team.

"Come on, let's go," I said.

Emma looked scared. "I can't face everybody! Not after my shoe flew off like that. It's so embarrassing!"

"I bet nobody even noticed," Zoe said. She started running and pulling Emma along with her.

"Thanks, girls," Coach Flores said, nodding to us. "You all played a good game today. I know it hurts to lose, but the Rams are a skilled team, and I know you played your best."

Coach Flores was one of those coaches who never got mad and who was always positive, no matter what. Other coaches might have barked at us for losing by one point, but not her.

She looked at Emma. "It looks like you had an equipment malfunction," she said. "Making sure our equipment is in good shape will guarantee that we *can* do our best. So try to get that problem fixed by the next practice, okay?"

Emma nodded, not looking at anyone else on the team. "Yes, Coach. It won't happen again."

Coach Flores smiled. "All right, then. Let's shake off this loss and get focused on our next game. Go, Kicks!"

"Go, Kicks!" we echoed, but without much enthusiasm. I could tell that everyone was bummed out by the loss.

"Yum Yum Yogurt?" I asked in a loud voice, and a few of the girls chimed in.

"Yeah!"

"Sure!"

"See you there!"

We usually went somewhere to eat after a game, whether we were celebrating a win or comforting one another after a loss. Our parents were used to this, so we quickly figured out that my mom would drop me and my friends off at the yogurt shop, and Jessi's dad would pick us all up.

Before I headed out for yogurt, though, there was one thing I had to do.

"Steven!" I called out, running toward him in the stands. He turned and smiled at me, waving the pom-poms.

"You are too funny," I said. "Thanks for being my personal cheerleader."

He grinned at me. "Sure. You're always at my games, when you can make it."

Cody was standing behind Steven, and I swear I saw him roll his eyes. I guess he wasn't into the cheerleading thing.

"We're going to Yum Yum. Wanna come?" I asked.

He shook his head. "Sounds good, but I've got to work on that science report. I put it off till the last minute."

"All right, then," I told him. "Maybe next time. Good luck!"

I jogged toward the parking lot, where Mom was waiting for us in front of our white minivan.

"No Maisie and Dad?" I asked.

"They took Dad's car, straight from Maisie's soccer practice," Mom reminded me. "And good thing too, because now I can fit everybody."

We all piled into the Marshmallow (that was our family's name for the minivan), and Mom drove us to the yogurt shop. I looked out the window as we rode, watching the feathery green leaves of the palm trees silhouetted against the bright blue sky.

Less than a year before, my family had moved to Southern California from Connecticut, and we might as well have moved from another planet. It was spring now, but in Connecticut there was still snow frozen to the ground in some places, and the temperatures hadn't climbed past 50 degrees yet. Here in California, I hadn't seen a single snowflake all winter, and the temperature almost always hovered around 70 degrees, no matter what time of year it was.

I missed the seasons, sometimes. My best friend, Kara, and I had just started to learn how to snowboard when I'd left. I missed the orange, yellow, and red leaves in the fall—but I didn't miss raking them up while Maisie ran through every leaf pile I'd collected, making more work for me. And the best thing about nice weather all year— soccer all year round!

We quickly got to Yum Yum Yogurt and piled out of the car. The place was pretty crowded for a Saturday afternoon, filled with other kids in team uniforms just like we were.

"I see a table!" Jessi cried. She shoved some crumpled-up bills into my hand. "Devin, get me a medium chocolate with the works, please."

"Everything? No way. That takes too long, and I can't do yours and mine at the same time," I protested.

"Fine! Just make it good!" Jessi called, making a beeline for the table.

I got in line behind Emma, Zoe, and Frida. Some more Kicks came in and got behind us: Grace, my co-captain; her friend Anjali, who had gorgeous, shiny dark hair; and freckle-faced Hailey. She was the newest member of the Kicks, in seventh grade just like me—and she was really good.

"Where's Jessi?" Hailey asked.

"Saving a table," I said. I looked across the room to where Jessi was sitting. "Looks like there's room for all of us."

I approached the yogurt bar and grabbed two medium cups. I filled one with vanilla for me, and one with chocolate for Jessi. I put mango, pineapple, and blueberries on mine. Jessi's got sprinkles, strawberries, walnuts, and breakfast cereal.

Pretty soon we were all sitting at the table, eating our yogurt and talking about the game.

"I've got to admit, they played a good game," Grace was saying. "Fair and square."

"Yeah, they've got some strong players and play well as a team," Hailey agreed, shaking her head.

Emma was looking down at her yogurt, stirring it over and over again with her spoon.

"Don't sweat it, Emma," Grace said. "We'll win next time."

Emma sighed. "I hope so."

"Cheer up, Emma," Jessi said, putting her arm around Emma's shoulders. Then her eyes got wide. "Look, there's Sebastian."

I followed her eyes to a table across the room. A family was sitting there: a mom, a dad, a little girl, and a boy who looked to be our age—a boy with wavy dark hair and darker eyes. He was laughing with his little sister.

"Sebastian?" I asked.

"Sebastian Delgado," Jessi explained. "He's new. I have a class with him. He's really nice and easy to talk to."

Hailey nodded. "Yeah, he is. He's in my French class."

"How do you say 'cute boy' in French?" Jessi asked.

Emma nudged her. "Jessi! Don't let Cody hear you say that."

Jessi shrugged. "Why not? Cody's not my boyfriend."

"Well, no, but . . ." Emma's voice trailed off.

There was an awkward silence for a few seconds, and then everyone started talking about soccer again. I got what Emma meant. I mean, Cody wasn't Jessi's boyfriend. Steven wasn't mine either. But still, we did things together. And when I finally felt like I was ready to have a boyfriend, it would probably be Steven. Especially after the amazing cheerleading he'd done for me that day!

I turned to Jessi. "We're still going to the mall with Cody and Steven tomorrow, right?"

Jessi nodded. "Yeah. Emma and Hailey are coming too. And Cody's bringing some guys from the Kangaroos."

Officially, every team at Kentville Middle School was called the Kangaroos. The girls' soccer team had always been known as the Kicks, for short.

Jessi smiled and waved at Sebastian, and he waved back. I couldn't help noticing that he had a really nice smile.

"I guess he is pretty cute," I whispered to Jessi.

"No kidding," Jessi said, and then she took another bite of her yogurt.

CHAPTER THREE

"Come on!" Cody grabbed Jessi by the arm. We were at the mall. "Let's try to run up the down escalator!"

Jessi shook her head and pulled her arm away from Cody. "We'll get kicked out by the security guards," she said, her voice crackling with irritation. She rolled her eyes. "Gosh, Cody, you can be so immature sometimes."

Steven looked at me, his eyebrows raised. I shrugged my shoulders awkwardly, not knowing what to say. Emma and Hailey were chatting with Daniel and José, two fellow Kangaroos who played with Steven and Cody. They didn't notice the tense exchange between Jessi and Cody.

"Come on!" I said, trying to change the subject. "Let's go to Sports World. Emma needs to try on some new cleats."

Emma sighed loudly. "Forget it. I tried on every pair of cleats there last week when I was with my mom. Like I told you, they're either too tight or too loose."

"Have you tried the Bia Force 3X's?" José asked her. "They mold to your feet. They are fantastic. I love mine."

Emma's face lit up. "You know, they didn't have them in stock when we were there. Maybe we can check to see if they're in now."

We went around to the up escalator (we didn't run up the down one like Cody had suggested), and I noticed that Jessi hung back to walk next to Hailey, leaving Cody with me and Steven.

Steven and I could tell that Jessi was aggravated, but Cody seemed clueless. He walked next to us, slurping loudly on the bright blue slushee he had gotten at a food court stand.

The bright blue matched Cody's eyes. He had wavy blond hair that always seemed to fall over his eyes, no matter how much he pushed it away. Steven was kind of opposite-looking, with dark eyes and short, spiky black hair.

Usually I had my long brown hair pulled into a ponytail, but today I'd worn it down. Since I had moved to California, I hadn't had to worry about blow-drying it as much. In Connecticut if you went out of the house with wet hair in March, your head would turn into a Popsicle. When my hair air-dried now, it had a nice wave and looked like I'd just come from the beach. The sun had also given my hair some blondish streaks. When I video chatted with Kara, she teased me about looking like a total California beach girl.

Inside Sports World, Emma and José made a beeline for the wall with all the cleats on display. Hailey began looking through a rack of soccer jerseys.

"Number thirteen, my favorite!" She pulled out the shirt, and then looked at the price tag and shook her head. "I'll have to ask for it as a birthday present. It's way more than my weekly allowance!"

Cody came strolling out of one of the aisles wearing a plaid golf hat with a pompom on the top.

"Golf, anyone?" he said in snooty voice. His lips were blue from the slushee, and he looked ridiculous.

Jessi began laughing so hard that I thought she was going to cry. But she composed herself.

"Yes, let's play a round and then have high tea," she joked back in a funny British accent.

They went back and forth, each being more ridiculous, and Steven, Hailey, Daniel, and I laughed along with them. Part of my laughter was relief. It made me feel tense to hang out with Jessi when she was so annoyed at Cody, so it was nice to see everyone having a good time and getting along.

It got even better when Emma and José came back from looking at cleats. Emma was smiling widely.

"They didn't have the Bia Force shoes in stock, but the guy said they could order them. He's pretty sure they'll work perfectly for me. The store will have the cleats in a couple of days, so there will be plenty of time for me to try them out and break them in before the next game," she said.

I clapped my hands together excitedly. "Emma, that's awesome! No more cleat malfunctions for you."

"I just want to put that whole embarrassing incident behind me!" Emma said forcefully. "It was almost worse than the time I scored a goal for the other team."

"I remember that," Daniel said. "That was one of the first games of the fall season, right?"

Emma nodded. "Yeah. It's how I knew I wasn't cut out to be a midfielder. Devin is the one who saw I had a talent for the goal, and she talked me into giving it a try."

"And you're a natural, Emma!" I said.

"Um, not when my cleat is flying off and hitting me in the head," Emma joked. "There's nothing natural about that!"

We all laughed, and I was glad that Emma seemed to be feeling better about the whole cleat disaster. Things were looking up!

We headed to the arcade next, and Jessi and Cody went straight for the Dance Party! machine. It was a game where you had to follow the arrows on the screen by hitting lighted up arrows with your feet on the floor. It got faster and faster as it went. I was terrible at it, but Jessi was a pro. Two people can play against each other side by side.

"I'm going to beat you this time, Jessi," Cody vowed. "I've been practicing."

"We'll see about that," Jessi said confidently as she put money into the machine.

The music started, slow at first but picking up speed. Jessi kept the pace, her feet moving like a blur on the pad, and Cody moved like lightning. Both of them were doing so great that a bunch of other kids gathered around to watch.

Jessi was undefeated. Cody had never been able to beat her before. But when the game ended, his score was 250 points higher.

"Ha! I told you I was going to win!" he yelled, and he put up a hand to high-five her.

Jessi slapped his hand, but her heart wasn't in it.

"Good job," she said, but I could tell that she wasn't happy with his reaction.

"Dude, not very sportsmanlike," Steven said to Cody.

Cody shrugged. "I was just joking around," he said. "It's not soccer. It's just some dumb dance game."

"Yeah, dumb," Jessi said, and she turned away from him. "I'm going to play Zombie Hunt. Emma, you wanna come with?"

Dance Party! was Jessi's favorite game, and Zombie Hunt was Emma's. It was kind of funny, because Emma loved all things cute and fluffy, but she could slay zombies in that video game like a champ.

I noticed that two of the kids who had been watching Jessi and Cody square off during the dance video game were whispering and pointing at Emma. One of them pulled out his phone and pointed. They both looked up at Emma and started laughing.

Nobody in our group seemed to notice. *What's going on?* I wondered. If they were laughing at my friend, I wanted to know why.

"What's so funny?" I asked as I walked over to them.

The one boy, who looked around ten, began to fidget nervously.

"It's just your friend," he said, pointing at Emma, who was talking to Jessi. "She's, like, famous on SnapFace."

He showed me his phone, and there was a picture of Emma at yesterday's game. It was taken right at the moment when her cleat had hit her. Her mouth was open and her tongue was sticking out in a really unflattering way. Someone had turned the photo into a meme. Written on it was, "Runaway Cleats!"

I gasped. "Where did this come from?"

He shrugged. "I don't know, but there's a bunch of them."

"Let me see," I demanded.

His hand shook a little as he searched on his phone. I realized I might be coming on too strong.

"It's okay." I smiled. "Emma's my friend, and I'm just protective of her. You didn't do anything wrong."

That relaxed him, and he began to talk.

"There's a ton of memes with your friend's picture on them," he said. "I saw them on SnapFace, InstaPhoto and TextFest."

He began pulling up photo after photo. One was a close-up of Emma's face with her tongue protruding. It looked like she was about to lick her cleat. That caption said, "The taste of deFEET."

"Where did these all come from?" I wondered out loud.

"Somebody probably used a meme generator to make them," the kid replied. "You can upload any photo and write a caption on it, and then share it on all different social media sites."

"Thanks for telling me," I told the kid. "Please do me a favor and don't like them or share them. That's a picture of my friend, and she's going to be really upset. Imagine if it was a photo of you."

He nodded, his eyes wide.

I walked back to the group, not knowing how I was going to break the news to Emma. I decided to be straightforward. "Rip the Band-Aid off quickly," my grandpa always said.

When I got there, Cody was on his knees, playfully begging Jessi to forgive him.

"I'm sorry," he pleaded. "I never thought I'd beat you at that game, ever. You're the best. It's like beating Lionel Messi in soccer. I got a little too excited."

I could see Jessi's face soften, and she gave a small smile. "Okay, fine. You're forgiven."

It was a cute moment, but I had to interrupt it to break the news to Emma. "Emma, I need to tell you something," I told her while everyone listened. "Someone was taking pictures of our game against the Rams. They took one of you with your cleat hitting your head, and turned it into a bunch of stupid Internet memes."

"What?" Emma asked, a look of surprise crossing her face. "Are you sure?"

I nodded. "I wish it weren't true," I said. "But that kid over there recognized you, and he showed me," I explained, pointing. "It's on SnapFace, InstaPhoto, Text-Fest, everywhere."

Emma gasped. "Let me see. No, I don't want to see." She shook her head. "No, I do. I mean, yes I do. Ugh! Just show me!"

Everyone got their phones out and searched.

"Oh no," Jessi groaned.

"Jeez." Steven shook his head.

Hailey sighed. "That's not nice."

Emma peered over Hailey's shoulder. "Oh my gosh! I look like a total dork."

Cody let out a loud laugh. "DeFEET. Get it?" he said as he chuckled.

Jessi whacked him on the arm. "What's wrong with you? Emma is upset."

Again Cody looked confused. "It's not a big deal. It's just a joke."

"You and your jokes," Jessi said, crossing her arms over her chest. "You need to get a better sense of humor."

I nudged Jessi. "Not helping!" I said as I looked at Emma's face. She looked like she might cry.

"I want to go home," Emma said, her voice shaking.

"We'll go with you." Jessi put an arm around her shoulder while very purposefully not looking at Cody.

Mrs. Kim had offered to drive us home. Emma texted her mom to pick us up early. Hailey was driving back with the boys. Her family and Steven's were good friends, and they lived on the same block.

"I'll see you later," I said to Steven.

He made a sad face. "I hope Emma is okay."

"Me too," I said.

When Mrs. Kim picked us up at the mall entrance, Emma immediately told her mom everything.

Mrs. Kim patted her daughter on the leg.

"We'll look into it as soon as we get home and see if there's anything we can do to get those pictures taken down," Mrs. Kim tried to reassure Emma. I could tell that Emma felt better just by talking with her mom, but I still felt really bad for her. I'd goofed up plenty of times in soccer. If someone had made a meme about it, I'd have wanted to crawl into a cave and never come out.

Later that night I video chatted with Kara and told her the entire story.

Kara frowned, her big blue eyes looking sad. "Poor Emma! She is such a sweetie!"

Kara had come out to visit me once since I'd moved to California, and she had gotten the chance to meet all my new friends.

"I know," I sighed. "Why her? She's always so cheerful and positive. But she's having a hard time being upbeat about this."

Kara shuddered. "Who can blame her? I wouldn't know

how to find the bright side either. I'd be totally embarrassed."

I remembered what Emma had said before the game and the whole cleat incident had happened.

"You know, before the game even started, Emma was trying to describe how much pressure there is on the goalie," I told Kara. "I'd never really thought about it before."

"You remember Julie, right?" Kara asked. She was on Kara's soccer team, the one I used to play on before I moved.

"Julie? Of course!" I answered. We had been friends.

"She got moved from defense to goal this past fall, and she had a tough time with it," Kara revealed. "She's really good, but she said the anxiety of it was what bothered her the most at first."

"What do you mean?" I asked.

"Julie said that as a defender, she might miss a tackle. It upset her, but it was easier to move on and not dwell on it because it wasn't so instant and game-changing as missing a goal," Kara explained.

I nodded thoughtfully. "Yeah, I get it. As a striker, if I miss a scoring chance, I just focus on catching the next one. The game isn't dramatically affected right away like it is when someone scores a goal."

"It really bothered Julie every time she let someone score," Kara said. "But eventually she got over it."

"How did she do that?" I asked, hoping it could be something that could help Emma too.

"She had a lot of talks with Coach," Kara said. "Coach gave her some breathing exercises to do and a mantra to chant before each game. It helped her get in the zone, she said."

"Hmmmm." I thought about that. Zoe had once taught me some relaxation techniques when I was having a hard time on the field. Maybe that could help Emma too.

"Do you know what exercises she used?" I asked Kara.

She shook her head. "No, but I'll find out and let you know."

I was finally understanding just how hard it was to be a goalie. If Emma's confidence had been hurting before, the online memes were going to make it worse. But now I had some ideas about how I could help get her back into the zone!

CHAPTER FOUR

When we moved to California, I started going to Kentville Middle School. It was pretty much like my old middle school back in Connecticut, except for the palm trees on the lawn. And the fact that we could eat lunch outside pretty much every day if we wanted to. And some kids wore flip-flops to school.

Otherwise, it was a lot like other schools, I guess. It had easy teachers and tough teachers. Interesting classes and boring classes. And at lunch, kids sat in groups: sports kids, drama kids, art kids, tech kids. During soccer season, members of the Kicks usually sat together.

When I got to the cafeteria on Monday for lunch, Emma was slouched in her seat. She had her big World Civ book open on the table, hiding her face.

"Um, are you studying?" I asked. "I didn't think we had a test today."

"We don't," she said. "I'm hiding."

"Hiding from what?" I asked.

"Yeah, what?" asked Jessi, as she, Zoe, and Frida took their seats at the table at the same time.

Before Emma could answer, a boy came up to our table. I knew his name was Brandon, but that was all I knew about him. He was in eighth grade.

He walked right over to Emma. "Oh, man. It really is you! You're famous! I love your memes."

"I don't know what you're talking about," Emma responded.

"The memes! Where that shoe is hitting you in the head! And you're making that face!" Brandon mimicked the face Emma had made in the photo. "Classic."

Emma looked really upset. Jessi spoke up.

"All right, Brandon. She said it wasn't her. Leave it alone," she said.

"But she's wearing a Kicks uniform in the picture!" Brandon protested. "Who else could it be?"

Jessie just glared at him, and he shrugged and walked away.

Zoe put a hand on Emma's shoulder. "Has this been going on all day?"

Emma nodded silently.

"That stinks," I said.

"I think there's a bright side to this," said Frida. Recently she had made friends with a retired movie star from the 1940s, and she'd started wearing her hair in old movie styles. Today her shiny auburn hair rippled down the sides of her face like waves.

"What bright side?" Jessi asked. "Emma is totally mortified."

"But she's a celebrity now," Frida said. "Seriously. Those memes have been shared thousands of times. Most people would pay a lot to have a meme go viral."

"If this is what it means to be a celebrity, then I don't want to be one!" Emma wailed. "It's hard enough being a tall, gangly girl who's constantly tripping over stuff. I don't want to be famous for that."

"I'm just saying," Frida went on, "that you could capitalize on this. Get an endorsement for shoelaces or something."

"Frida, when was the last time you saw a commercial for shoelaces?" Zoe asked.

"Hey, I'm trying to think out of the box," Frida told her. "It's not like the memes are going to go away. Emma might as well make lemonade out of lemons."

"I hate lemonade," Emma replied. "And I hope you're wrong about the memes not going away. They're just a constant reminder that I lost the game for us."

Everyone was quiet for a minute. I could understand how much it would hurt if a meme went around showing me missing a game-winning goal. I'd be miserable!

"Don't worry, Emma," I said. "I'm sure this will blow over soon."

But Emma still looked worried, and she barely ate her

lunch. (Okay, when I say "barely," I mean she ate only her sandwich, cookie, and banana. She left half a snack bag of potato chips and a squeezable yogurt. Normally she finishes it all. It takes a lot of food to fuel my supertall friend who never stops moving.) I hoped practice would take her mind off the stupid memes.

When school was over, the Kicks all headed for the girls' locker room by the gym and changed into our practice clothes. Then we walked over to our field. Jessi was cracking everyone up with her impression of Mrs. Clarke, her algebra teacher.

"You don't have to be *afraid* of polynomials," Jessi was saying in a high-pitched voice. "They're just equations, not *scary monsters!*"

"I swear, she talks to us like we're in kindergarten sometimes," Zoe agreed.

Everyone was laughing but Emma. She stared down at her feet as she walked.

Along the way, we passed the boys practicing on the school field. Back in the fall we'd been jealous that they had such a great field to practice on. But now our field was even better, thanks to Sally Lane, who owned the sporting goods store in town. We had brand-new sod, professional goalposts and nets, and all new soccer balls and cones.

We all started stretching as soon as we got to the field, waiting for Coach Flores to start practice. After I stretched, I started dribbling a soccer ball. I was looking forward to practice. It felt good to be up and moving, after being stuck in school all day.

When Coach Flores appeared, Emma ran up to her. Emma looked pretty upset. I was curious, so I dribbled closer to hear what she was saying. (And yes, I know that's eavesdropping, but I was starting to get really worried about Emma.)

"It's just, I think maybe I need a break from the goal," Emma was saying. "We've already got Zarine. I bet somebody else would be good at it too."

"*You're* really good," Coach Flores told her. "I don't want to see you give up because of one accident." Emma nodded but still looked sad. Coach Flores motioned for her to start walking. "Come on," she said. "I have special plans for today's practice."

I quickly dribbled back to the rest of the team. Everyone gathered around Coach when she approached.

"All right, team. I know we had a tough loss this weekend," she began.

Everybody nodded and murmured in agreement.

"It was an especially tough loss for one of our goalies, Emma," Coach Flores went on, and I saw Emma's face turn bright red. "It got me thinking that most of you have never played goalie before. All the positions on the team come with their own kind of pressure, but I think goalies are under more pressure than anybody else."

"It's true." Zarine spoke up. "It's like you feel totally responsible when the team loses."

"Exactly," Coach Flores said. "Even though every member of the Kicks is equally responsible for our team's performance, no matter if we win or lose."

Grace clapped. "That's right!"

"So today we're all going to do goalie drills," Coach Flores said.

A few of the girls groaned.

"See, that's exactly why I'm doing this," Coach said. "Everyone needs to know what our goalies go through. So everybody, grab a ball and line up!"

We quickly lined up on the field.

"Goalies have to be really skilled with their hands," Coach said. "For this drill I want you to walk around the perimeter of the field bouncing the ball from one hand to the other. If you drop the ball, dive for it and recover it with both hands."

It seemed like a simple enough drill, but we quickly learned that catching a ball one-handed isn't as easy as it looks, especially when you're moving. Soon girls were diving onto the grass, trying to catch their dropped balls. I dropped mine twice before I made it all the way around the field.

"Great!" Coach said. "Now everyone find a partner and stand twenty yards apart."

Jessi and I ran out onto the field together (she's almost always my partner when we drill) and faced off at twenty yards apart, using the yard lines to guide us. Coach Flores demonstrated some goalie throws for us.

One was called an underarm roll, where you roll the ball along the grass to a player near you. The other was a one-handed overhead throw, which was better for longer distances but required a lot more precision. For a few minutes we took turns throwing the ball back and forth to each other.

Next Coach Flores had us line up in front of the goal. She sent Zarine to the goal first. Grace took a shot at the goal, and Zarine caught it. Then Zarine ran to the back of the line and it was Grace's turn at the goal. We kept going down the line until everyone had a turn.

When it was my turn, I kicked the ball high and left and sent it whizzing past Frida. I jogged past her on my way to the goal.

"Couldn't you have gone easy on me?" Frida teased.

I took my place at the goal. Jessi had the ball. I knew for a fact that *she* wouldn't go easy on me. And she didn't. She zigged and zagged across the field so that I didn't know where to go. I was on the left side of the goal when she took her shot, sending it skidding across the grass to the right. I ran as fast as I could and then made a mighty dive, determined to get the ball. *Whomp!* I got it, but face-planting in the grass was never fun. I brushed dirt off my knees as I took my place at the back of the line.

It was Emma's turn to take a shot next, and she managed to get one past Jessi. Everybody cheered for her. Then at the goal, she stopped a ball from Jade.

"See, you're a natural," I told Emma as she moved to the back of the line. But my usually sunny friend did not return my smile. She just nodded.

We had a short scrimmage after that, and during the practice game Coach had each and every one of us take turns in front of the goal. Things got pretty hectic, because Coach kept switching positions every few minutes. I didn't mind so much. It definitely wasn't a boring practice!

By the time Coach Flores called for us to stretch and cool down, we were all sweaty messes. Zoe put an arm around Emma (which she had to reach up to do, because Zoe is so much shorter).

"Mad respect, Em," Zoe said. "It's pretty scary in front of that goal, with the ball coming right at you . . ."

"I could never do it," Frida added. "You have to stay so focused!"

"This is exactly why I need to take a break from goal," Emma said.

I acted surprised. "Emma, no! You can't! We need you!"

"The team has Zarine," she replied. "You guys will be fine without me."

Coach Flores walked up to us. "How are you doing, Emma?" she asked.

Emma shrugged. "Okay, I guess. I still think I need a break from goal."

Coach nodded. "I understand. I don't want to pressure you. Why don't you sleep on it?"

"Sure," Emma said with a nod.

Coach turned to the team. "Great practice, everybody! Have a good night!"

We walked back to the locker room.

"Emma, you can't give up the goal," Zoe said. "Is that stupid meme bothering you? Is that what this is about?"

"Maybe," Emma said. She sighed. "I don't know."

I had never seen Emma like this—and I hated it! I wanted my goofy, eternally positive friend back.

But something told me that getting her back wasn't going to be easy.

CHAPTER FIVE

The next day at lunch I almost walked right by Emma without recognizing her. Today, instead of covering her face with her World Civ book, she had put on a baseball cap and pulled it down over her face.

"Is that you, Emma?" I asked, peering under the brim of her hat.

Emma sighed and looked up. "You spotted me. I thought I could be invisible."

Just then Mrs. Castillo, the assistant principal, walked by. "No hats in school!" her voice rang out. "Please take it off, Emma."

Emma shrugged as she removed the cap from her head. "It wasn't working anyway."

As she stuffed her hat into her backpack, I asked, "Are people still talking about the memes?"

"Oh, yeah. In fact, in homeroom this morning Amy

Rodriquez showed me a new one. It had that stupid picture of me. This one just says 'MAJOR FAIL' in capital letters." Emma crossed her arms on the table and put her head down.

I shook my head. "That's awful. I'm sorry, Emma."

Jessi came over, carrying her lunch tray.

"Why aren't you guys at our regular table? I couldn't find you!"

"Emma is trying to be invisible," I said as I sat down and got my lunch out of my backpack.

"Um, you're going to need to work on that, Emma," Jessi said. "I can totally see you. You might want to consider Harry Potter's Invisibility Cloak."

A couple of kids from the next table pointed at Emma and laughed. Emma saw them and groaned.

"I'm ready to transfer to Hogwarts," she sighed.

Frida and Zoe had found us and were sitting down too.

"Why the table change?" Frida wondered.

"I'm trying to disappear," Emma admitted. "But it didn't work. I had a hat on but Mrs. Castillo made me take it off. I don't like the fame, Frida. If you want to swap your face with mine on all those memes, feel free."

"It will blow over," Zoe said encouragingly. "You've got to wait it out."

Emma looked miserable. Jessi and I exchanged glances, and I could tell we were both thinking the same thing: subject change!

"So my mom and dad were talking about baby names

the other day," Jessi began. Her mom was having a baby. At first Jessi, who was an only child, hadn't been too happy about it. She came around to accepting it after Emma and I gave her a crash course in babysitting. It turned out that Jessi was a natural with little kids. Knowing that had made her feel a lot better about becoming a big sister.

"My father wants to name the baby Clarence if it's a boy." Jessi shook her head. "It was my great-grandfather's name. But I think it's way too old-fashioned. Can you imagine looking at a tiny little baby and calling him *Clarence?*"

"The name 'Clarence' has *gravitas*," Frida said in her dramatic way, emphasizing the word "gravitas."

"It's got what now?" Emma asked, frowning.

"Yeah, who is Gravitas?" Zoe wondered.

"'Gravitas,'" Frida said solemnly, looking at each of us one by one. Our actor friend knew how to ham it up. "Means 'dignified and serious.'"

"That just proves my point!" Jessi exclaimed. "What is dignified and serious about a baby who poops in diapers?"

I laughed. "But he won't be a baby forever!"

"That's true, but I'm hoping for a baby sister anyway," Jessi said.

I rolled my eyes. "Baby sisters aren't all that great sometimes, believe me," I said, thinking of my little sister, Maisie, who knew exactly how to push all of my buttons.

"The trick with sisters," a boy's voice suddenly said, "is to get them to do what you want. My little sister thinks that weeding the garden is the most fun thing in the world. It used to be my chore, and I pretended it was so much fun, that she begged to do it. Now I'm off the hook."

I looked up as I felt Jessi's elbow dig into my side. It was Sebastian, the new, cute boy whom Jessi had pointed out at Yum Yum Yogurt.

"I'll have to remember that," Jessi said as she smiled at him.

While Jessi was talking, Emma put her head on the table and covered her head with her hands.

Sebastian raised his eyebrows. "What's wrong with her?"

"I'm invisible. You can't see me," Emma said, her voice muffled.

"Hey, you're Emma! I was at the game last Saturday. That was a spectacular save you made in the first half," he said.

Emma lifted her head up. "That's not what I'm being remembered for from that game."

"Oh, you're talking about all those memes, huh?" Sebastian asked. Emma nodded her head sadly. "The way you play, I wouldn't worry about it. Soon you'll have lots more memes about what an amazing player you are."

"Thanks," Emma said, and I saw her smile for the first time that day.

Sebastian glanced at Jessi. "So, Jessi, a bunch of us are going to the movies on Sunday. Do you want to come?"

"That depends," Jessi said. "What are you seeing?"

"We want to check out the latest Star Warriors movie,"

Sebastian said. "The galactic queen is supposed to defeat the evil alien warlord in this one. . . . Sorry, do I sound too much like a nerd?"

"A little, but that's okay. I like to nerd out over Star Warriors too," Jessi admitted.

"Yeah, and you should see her when *The Sunshine Puppies* comes on!" Emma joked.

The Sunshine Puppies was a kids' show that Jessi had watched when she was younger and that she still liked now. She was really looking forward to watching it again with her new sibling.

"I told you, I'm not afraid to admit my love of *The Sunshine Puppies*," Jessi said, laughing.

"It's my sister's favorite show," Sebastian said, and he shook his head. "Oh, man! Now I'm going to have the theme song stuck in my head."

Jessi laughed and burst into song. "What's better than sunshine? Sunshine . . . puppies . . ."

Sebastian put his hands over his ears. "Nooooo!" he joked. Then took his hands away from his ears and got serious. "So, what's your number? I'll text you the details. We were planning on going to the Sunday matinee."

While Jessi and Sebastian traded info, Zoe looked at me and made a questioning face. I returned her look with one of my own.

After Sebastian left, I asked Jessi, "What about Cody?"

"What about him?" Jessi said as she picked up her slice of pizza and took a bite.

"Well, you know. . . . You, me, Steven, and Cody all hang out together," I reminded her.

"Yeah, but why would that mean that I can't hang out with Sebastian, too?" Jessi asked. "It's not like Cody's my boyfriend."

"I mean, I know you guys aren't dating, but isn't he more than just a friend?" Zoe asked, sounding skeptical. "Cody did take you to the fall dance."

"It was just a dance, Zoe." Jessi sounded irritated. "It's not like we got married."

"Yes, but we all thought you guys were sort of . . . together," Emma added.

"We are not dating. We never were," Jessie insisted.

"I get it, I guess, but it's just kind of strange to see you going to the movies now with Sebastian," Zoe pointed out.

Jessi shook her head. "Listen, guys, it's no big deal. Sometimes I go to the movies with you, Zoe, and sometimes I go with Devin. It's the same thing."

It was obvious that Jessi didn't think it was a big deal, but I suspected that Cody might think it was a big deal. And that could cause problems with our whole arrangement with Cody and Steven, who were best friends.

"Does this mean we're not going to hang out with Cody and Steven together anymore?" I asked.

"Why would it?" Jessi replied. "We're all friends. This doesn't change anything."

I felt a little better. Maybe I was getting too wound up. I mean, I really liked Steven, but how could we spend time together if Jessi started preferring Sebastian over Cody? That would mean that Steven and I would have to start hanging out without them.

The thought of that kind of freaked me out a little bit. I always said that my parents wouldn't let me date, but deep down I knew that I wasn't ready to date either. Dating meant holding hands and stuff, and the thought of that just made me feel nervous. When the four of us hung out together, I didn't have to worry about that. But now . . .

Then I heard my grandmother's voice in my mind. "Cross that bridge when you come to it." Grandma always had a wise saying for me whenever I had a problem. She and my grandpa had just recently come for a visit from Connecticut, so most of her sayings were fresh in my mind.

And it was good advice. For all I knew, everything would work out just fine. So I decided to not stress about it, and focus on eating my lunch instead.

My mom had made this awesome chicken salad with walnuts and dried cranberries that she had stuffed into a whole wheat wrap. She was totally into us all eating healthfully, and I had to say, I really liked just about everything she made. My sister, Maisie, on the other hand, loved to complain about her food all the time. But she still ate it anyway.

As I chewed, I saw Emma slump in her chair again. She had cheered up a bit after Sebastian's compliment, but now she seemed back to being down on herself.

"What's wrong?" I said after I swallowed.

"I'm still having trouble getting back into the confidence zone," she said. She twisted her napkin nervously, leaving little pieces of white dots all over the table. "I know Coach Flores told me to think about it, but I've made up my mind. I'm going to take a break from being goalie."

My jaw dropped. I had really thought that with a little time, Emma would get back into the zone. Would the Kicks be able to win without her in front of the goal?

CHAPTER SIX

Saturday morning dawned bright and sunny, and I jumped out of bed feeling great. We had an away game that day, with the Rancho Verdes Vipers.

I dressed in my soccer uniform and bounded downstairs. Mom was drinking a smoothie, Dad was sipping his coffee, and Maisie was coloring a big piece of poster board on the kitchen table.

"Oatmeal's in the Crock-Pot," Mom said. "I put dried apricots in it."

"Awesome!" I said, and I meant it. In my mom's world dried apricots were usually for dessert. But they were super-yummy in oatmeal.

I helped myself to a bowl and sat down at the table.

"Whatcha making, Maisie?" I asked my little sister.

She put down the marker in her hand and held up the sign. It read GO, KANGAROOS! and she had drawn a really good picture of a kangaroo kicking a soccer ball.

"Awesome!" I said.

"Is everything 'awesome' today?" Dad asked.

"I guess it is," I replied. "You guys are all coming to the game, right?"

"Of course," Dad said.

"It's a beautiful day for a game. Plus we're playing against the Rancho Verde Vipers," I said. "They're the first team we beat in the fall."

"I remember," Mom said. "That was the first game where Emma played goalie. Your team really started coming together after that."

I frowned. "Yeah, well, it doesn't look like Emma wants to be a goalie anymore."

Mom and Dad looked shocked. "Why not?" Mom asked.

Then I realized I hadn't even told them about the meme. "It's because of our last game, when her cleat fell off," I said. "Somebody got a photo of it, and it turned into a meme. A bunch of memes, actually."

Maisie giggled. "I know. They're so funny!"

Mom and I both looked at Maisie. "*You* saw the memes?" we asked at the same time.

Maisie shrugged. "Kyle Miller showed it to everybody at school on his phone."

Mom started talking really fast, like her head might explode. "For one thing, there is a no-phone policy in your school, Maisie, so I will certainly be speaking with Principal Chen about that. And I can't believe that poor

Emma is the subject of a meme. Do her parents know about this?"

"I know she told her mom," I said.

Mom got up and took her phone off the charging station. "And how do I find these memes?"

"Look up, 'the taste of dafeet,'" Maisie said, and then started giggling.

"Maisie, this isn't funny!" I said. "This is Emma. You love Emma, right?"

Maisie nodded.

"Well, these memes are making her cry," I said. "She doesn't think it's funny."

Maisie got a sad look on her face when she realized how upset Emma was.

Mom was scrolling through her phone. "Poor Emma! There must be some way to get these off the Internet."

"I'm afraid that's nearly impossible," Dad chimed in. "But there should be a way of making sure nobody uses those memes to tease Emma in school."

"I'll talk to Emma's mom. She should be at the game," Mom said.

I wondered for a second if I had done the right thing by telling my mom. Emma had been so upset about the memes. Surely, even if her parents couldn't stop the memes, they could at least help her deal with what was going on.

A few minutes later we were all in the Marshmallow, headed to Rancho Verde. It was a short drive along the

freeway, and we quickly arrived at the middle school soccer field. The home team side was decked out with green
and yellow balloons, the colors of the Vipers.

That was why I always loved it when Kicks fans brought
signs and wore blue and white, Kicks colors. When I was
zooming down the field, trying to get to the other team's
goal, it gave me confidence to see blurs of blue and white
in the stands.

I gave Maisie a hug. "Thanks for making the sign. It's . . ."

"Awesome. I know," Maisie said, and then she stuck her
tongue out at me. I did the same to her and then jogged
onto the field to join the team.

It was early, and only a few members of the team had
arrived. One of them was Emma, and I saw her talking to
Coach Flores. I jogged up to them.

"I'm sorry I can't convince you, Emma," she said. "But I
want you to be happy on this team. How would you feel
about being a defender?"

Emma nodded. "I think I can give it a try."

"Great!" Coach Flores said. "But you'll need to be on
your toes, just like you were in front of the goal. The
Vipers' offense has gotten a lot better."

Emma nodded. "I won't let you down." She pointed
down to her cleats. "And neither will my laces."

Coach Flores walked away. "Switching to defense?" I
asked Emma.

"Yes, and I feel great!" Emma said. "I'm out of the goal
zone and into the no-pressure zone!"

"Well, I wouldn't exactly say it's a no-pressure zone," I told her, but Emma actually looked sort of happy for the first time in a week, so I didn't say anything more. She would remember soon enough what it was like out on the field.

Then we heard Grace's voice. "Sock swap time!"

The sock swap was a Kicks tradition that Jessi and I had started last fall. Before each game everybody on the team sat in a circle. Each person took off one sock and passed it to the girl on her left. So we each ended up wearing two different socks. It was fun because we all wore socks with different-colored stripes or patterns.

It was a silly tradition, but it had helped us bond as a team. Now we did the swap, and then lined up as Coach Flores called out positions. Zarine would take the goal; Emma would take defense with Frida and Anjali; Grace and Gabriela would play midfield; and Hailey, Zoe, and I would start as strikers. That left Jessi on the bench, but I knew she wouldn't be there for long. Coach Flores was always switching up players to give everyone a fair chance to play.

Hailey faced off with one of the Vipers for the first ball. She got control of it and started taking it down the field. Zoe and I flanked her on either side.

The last time we had played the Vipers, their defense had been weak—but they'd gotten a lot better. I had a player covering me closely, and I could see that Zoe was blocked on her side of the field. Hailey had nobody to pass to.

I started running toward Zoe, bringing the Vipers defense with me. Now they were clustered around me and Zoe, giving Hailey a path to the goal, and she took it. She zipped down the field and kicked the ball high into the goal—almost too high, I thought, expecting it to fly over the net. The Vipers goalie jumped up but couldn't reach it, and the ball dropped over her head and into the goal.

"Yes!" I cheered. The game had just started, and we were already ahead. I high-fived Zoe and Hailey as we jogged back into position. The Vipers got tough after that, and for most of the half we traded the ball back and forth. One of their strikers got past Frida and lobbed a shot at the goal, but Zarine stopped it.

The next time we had control of the ball, Hailey passed it to Zoe. She zigzagged between the Vipers at top speed—Zoe's specialty. But one of the defenders broke off and charged at her. Zoe quickly passed the ball to me before the defender could get her.

It was one of those perfect setups. I stopped the ball with my foot and then *wham!* sent it spiraling across the grass. The Vipers' goalie dove and missed it. Now we were up 2–0!

Near the end of the half, the Vipers got within goal range again. One of their players kicked the ball high, and Zarine jumped up and caught it. When she came down, her right foot landed sideways.

"You all right, Zarine?" Coach Flores called out, and

Zarine nodded that she was fine. But when the half ended just a minute later, Zarine came limping off the field.

"I think I twisted it, Coach," she said.

"Let's get you to the medic," Coach Flores said, linking arms with her. Then she nodded to me. "Devin, suit up! You're on goal next half."

"Me?" I blurted out, a little surprised.

But Coach was already shuffling Zarine away.

A bunch of thoughts were filling my head. *How am I supposed to suit up? Can I really play goal? Why did Coach pick me?*

Emma ran up to me. "Here, Devin. You can use my stuff." She led me to the bench and gave me goalie gloves, knee guards, and elbow guards. I started to put them on.

"How'd it go on defense?" I asked. I had been so focused on trying to score in the first half, I hadn't really paid attention to Emma's play.

Emma shrugged. "Not bad. But I'm not used to all that running. At least I didn't trip or anything."

Once I had the pads and gloves on, Emma slipped a head guard over my hair. "There you go. You look just like a goalie!" she said.

"I feel like a knight in armor," I said. "How do you move in all this stuff?"

Frida, who had been watching the whole scene, chimed in. "Did you say a knight in armor? That's an excellent idea," she said. "I am Frida the Bold, brave knight of defense! It has a ring to it, right?"

I couldn't answer, because Coach Flores had come back and was giving us the lineup for the second half. She put Jessi on the field as a striker and mixed up some of the other players. She left Emma and Frida on defense.

Before I knew it, I was standing in position in front of the goal. It seemed so much bigger than I'd remembered. *Just stay focused,* I told myself. *Keep your eye on the ball.*

I looked for the ball and saw that it was controlled by a Viper speeding down the field. Our midfielders were nowhere near her. When she got into the defensive zone, Emma ran up to her and got the ball, sending a beautiful punt to Grace in midfield.

"Thanks, Emma!" I called out to her, and she turned back to me and grinned.

"I punt all the time as goalie. It comes in handy out here," she said back.

I did feel grateful to Emma; if she hadn't intercepted that ball, I would have had to defend the goal for the very first time. And frankly, the thought made my stomach flip-flop a little.

I kept my eyes locked on the ball. A few minutes later two Vipers forwards were aggressively passing the ball back and forth. As they got closer, I saw Frida charge them.

"Stand back, intruders!" she yelled (in character as Frida the Bold, I assumed), but when she went for the ball, one Viper forward passed it to the other Viper forward, and before I knew it, the ball was flying toward the goal.

The ball was coming hard to the right of me, and I dove

for it—I really did!—but it whizzed past me and hit the net. The ref's whistle blew.

"It's okay, Devin!" Emma called out to me. "That was a tough one!"

For the first time, I knew exactly how Emma felt. The score was Kicks 2, Vipers 1, and it was my fault. It didn't matter that Frida hadn't been able to defend the goal for me. That ball had been sent to me, only me, and I had failed to block it.

It wasn't a great feeling. In fact, it felt like a punch in the gut. I steeled myself, put my hands on my knees, and focused on the game. I tried to tune out everything else.

I wasn't going to let it happen again.

And the next time the ball came to me, I didn't. I caught one ball that was kind of an easy lob, and I sent a low ball to Frida with one, strong kick. I was feeling pretty good—until I was taken off guard by one of the Vipers who faked right and sent a ball to my left. I couldn't get there in time, and the score was now tied!

I wasn't thinking about the two goals I had stopped. All I could think about were the two goals I had let get past me. I was starting to lose focus. But Jessi scored to put us in the lead again, and thankfully, a few minutes later the game was over.

I ran to Emma and hugged her. "Emma! That was intense!"

Emma nodded. "I know, right?"

"I finally get it," I said. "I totally didn't realize the pressure you were under."

"It's okay," Emma said. "And anyway, you did great."

I shook my head. "Not as good as you would have, Emma."

"You're just saying that so you don't have to be goalie anymore," she told me, and I could tell she was only half-teasing.

"No, seriously. I've seen you block shots way better than I did today," I said. "My mom was just saying that the Kicks really started coming together when you started playing goal."

Emma didn't say anything. It looked like she was thinking. Then we both got swept away into our team's victory cheers. Afterward Mom, Dad, and Maisie came down to the field.

"That was a surprise," Dad said. "How'd you like playing goal?"

"I'd rather be running and scoring," I admitted. "Honestly, I don't know if Coach was testing me out or if she'll put somebody else on next week."

Mom hugged me. "Well, you did a great job."

The rest of the day was a typical postgame Saturday, and we all went to a burrito place for lunch. At home, I did some schoolwork. Then I got on my computer and typed "goalie confidence" to see what would come up. I still wanted to help Emma get back in front of the goal— and if she didn't, I knew I'd have to be prepared if Coach kept me there.

I found a lot of blogs and comments on chat sites, with

goalies talking about the pressure they were under. There was a long and boring article with a meditation for goalies. Then I saw something cool.

It's Goalie-Palooza Time! Register Now!

It turned out that Goalie-Palooza was this nationwide one-day festival just for goalies. Goalies could go and compete at different age levels, plus show off their special goalie skills. There would be vendors selling goalie gear and merchandise, plus food and music.

I clicked through and saw that there was one happening soon, and just a few towns away! I started to get excited.

Emma had been born to be a goalie. I knew it in my bones. And being around other goalies might be just the thing to get her back in front of the net.

I knew what I had to do—I had to get Emma to Goalie-Palooza!

CHAPTER SEVEN

The next day I got a text from Jessi.

Come to the movie with me and Sebastian.

Who else is going? I texted back.

Luke and Isaac and I think Mary who plays basketball.

I hesitated. I didn't know any of these kids very well, but I knew they were all pretty nice. I did want to see the movie, and it wasn't like anyone else had asked me to go. Like Steven, for example.

K. I texted. What time?

My dad and I will pick you up at 2.

Of course I had to clear it with my parents, but they were just fine with it after they made sure I had no more homework. One of my deals with them was that I had to get As and Bs if I wanted to keep playing soccer, and since *nothing* was going to stop me from playing soccer, ever, I made sure to do all my homework and studying on time.

Jessi's dad came at two as promised and drove us to the mall. Along the way we mostly talked about the game against the Vipers, because even though I had a lot of questions about Sebastian, I didn't want to ask them in front of Mr. Dukes.

When we got to the mall, we took the escalator up to the second floor.

"So, do you know these friends of Sebastian's?" I asked Jessi.

She shrugged. "Sort of. Luke's in one of my classes. But if Sebastian likes them, they must be cool."

"Yeah, I guess so," I said, but I couldn't help thinking that Jessi sounded, like, really into Sebastian when she said it.

Then I heard Sebastian call out to us.

"Jessi! Devin! Over here!"

The mall was pretty crowded with shoppers, but we spotted Sebastian along with two boys and a girl standing by the theater entrance.

"Are they in . . . costume?" I asked.

Jessi grinned. "Yeah, cool!"

As she ran toward them, I tried to process what I was seeing.

Isaac, a short chubby kid, was wearing a brown fur vest and had horns on his head. Luke, a tall kid with glasses, was wearing all black with a cape, and a patch over one eye, which was a little awkward because of the glasses. Mary was wearing silver leggings and a silver top with puffy sleeves. Her brown hair was in a ponytail high on her head, and actual lights were weaved into the ponytail and flickered on and off. Sebastian had on black pants tucked into knee-high boots, along with a gray T-shirt under a black vest.

"Sebastian! You didn't tell me you were getting dressed up," Jessi said.

"I didn't want to scare you off," he said. "I mean, you're an athlete, so I thought maybe you would think I was a geek or something. Which I am, but . . . you know."

"No way! It's so cool!" Jessi said. "Right, Devin?"

I kind of felt like Jessi was putting me on the spot. I mean, I appreciated it whenever anybody put effort into something, and these guys had all obviously worked really hard to make these costumes. I didn't think it was something I would ever do, but I did think it was cool that they were so dedicated to their fandom.

"Yeah," I said, because it seemed like the right thing to say. "Totally cool."

Jessi pointed at Sebastian. "Benz Mordo, chief of the rebels."

Then Luke. "Lord Orfeo of the Dark Galaxy."

Then Mary. "Admiral Zeta of the resistance."

Then she looked at Isaac. "I forget. Who are you supposed to be?"

"I am a hobalur from the Dwarf Planet Cronus," Isaac replied. "From the second movie. A minor character, at best, but one with whom I resonate quite strongly."

I nodded. "Yup," I said, not sure how to comment on that.

"So, I hear it's a pretty good movie," Jessi remarked.

"Oh, it is," Sebastian replied.

"You saw it already?" Jessi asked.

Luke piped up. "Three times. It came out Friday, so we went to the Friday night show, a matinee yesterday, and then again last night."

"Wow, you guys are really into Star Warriors," I remarked. I looked at Jessi, expecting for her to make some kind of joke about it, because she had never been into this sci-fi stuff before. But she was just looking at Sebastian and smiling in a goofy way.

"We'd better go in, so we can get some good seats," Isaac said.

"Fine, but I need candy," Mary said.

We followed everyone into the theater. Jessi and I started walking toward the box office.

"We got our tickets already," Sebastian said, holding up his phone to show us his ticket app. "We'll wait for you."

So Jessi and I got into the ticket line—and right in front of us were Cody and Steven!

They spotted us first.

"Jessi! I didn't know you were coming here," Cody said.

"Well, I didn't know *you* were coming here either," Jessi replied. "You didn't ask me."

"Yeah, well, it was kind of last-minute," Cody said.

"Are you seeing Star Warriors?" Steven asked. "We could all sit together."

There was an awkward silence for a moment. I couldn't even meet Jessi's eyes.

How are we supposed to deal with this? I wondered.

Jessi handled it directly. "That would be really nice, normally, but we came with those guys." She motioned toward Sebastian and the others.

"Those guys? Do they know it's not Halloween?" Cody asked.

"Of course they do. They're dressed like characters from the movie," Jessi snapped.

I looked at Steven. "Listen, we made plans with those guys first. I hope you understand," I said. And then I repeated what Jessi had said. "You know, if you had asked . . ."

Steven nodded. "Hey, it's cool. We'll see you in there."

I nodded back, relieved that Steven wasn't making a big deal of it. We started talking about regular stuff, but I noticed Jessi and Cody had stopped speaking.

Jessi and I got our tickets, then got bottles of water and a large popcorn to split. Then we met back up with Sebastian and his friends and found seats.

Cody and Steven were already seated, all the way up in the back row. Sebastian and the others headed for a row in the middle of the theater.

"Optimum viewing level," Isaac remarked, even though nobody had asked why we were sitting there.

There was plenty of time before the movie started. Sebastian and his friends started talking about their favorite characters in the Star Warriors movies and making jokes. I found myself talking to them instead of watching the boring programming that was usually up on the screen before the previews started.

Then my phone vibrated. It was a text from Steven.

What's up with Jessi? Doesn't she like Cody anymore?

Whoa. I wasn't sure how to answer that.

I don't know, I replied. **Ask Jessi.**

You're her friend. What's going on?

I took a page from Jessi's playbook. **Jessi and Cody are just friends. What's the big deal?**

His response surprised me. **Are we just friends?**

My hands suddenly felt clammy, and I had to wipe them on my jeans so I could text back.

Well, you know I can't date, I typed, feeling grateful that I could use my parents as an excuse. The fact was, I wasn't sure if I could handle dating Steven for real. Not right then, anyway.

I know, he texted back. **But you know what I mean.**

I didn't know what to say. I mean, I did like Steven as *more* than a friend. At least I thought I did. Right then I wasn't even sure what that meant.

Words were failing me. I scrolled through my emojis. I chose a blushing emoji, sent it, and then instantly regretted it.

Just then the words "DON'T TEXT DURING THE MOVIE" appeared on the screen, and I shut down my phone. Jessi turned to me.

"Who were you texting?" she asked.

"Steven," I replied, and that was all I said. I couldn't talk about how awkward everything was, here in the movie theater, sitting next to a guy dressed like a space creature.

I was relieved when the movie started and I could forget about dating and what was happening with Jessi and Cody. The movie was good—really good—although I didn't think I would ever be inspired to dress up like one of the characters.

When we left the theater, there was no sign of Cody or Steven. I didn't get a chance to talk to Jessi about the texts that Steven had sent me, because her dad was already waiting for us outside.

"How was the movie?" Mr. Dukes asked as we got into the car.

"Awesome," Jessie replied.

"Good," I said, but inside I was thinking of a totally different word.

Awkward!

CHAPTER EIGHT

Thankfully, the awkward didn't last. That Monday at school Steven walked with me from World Civ to our eighth-period English class like we usually do.

"The movie had cool special effects," Steven said. "But it kind of lost me on the whole evil-twin thing. I didn't know who was who."

"Me too!" It felt good to talk about the movie with someone who wasn't a total fanatic. "Did Ambassador Rowan die, or her evil twin?"

Steven laughed. "I have no idea!"

He didn't mention our texts, or ask me any more questions about Jessi. We walked together to class on Tuesday, too, and everything was starting to feel normal again.

I had more important things to focus on, anyway. Like getting Emma to Goalie-Palooza!

My aim at lunch that day was to invite myself over to

her house. I wanted to convince her to give Goalie-Palooza a try, and I figured she'd be more comfortable in her own home, instead of asking her in the cafeteria.

"Want to hang after school today at your house?" I asked her. "Since there's no soccer practice?"

Her eyes brightened. "Cool! You can come home with me."

After school Emma's mom picked us up.

"I'm glad you're coming over, Devin," Mrs. Kim said as she glanced at me in the rearview mirror. "I've got a surprise for Emma, and I think you'll be able to help me with it."

"Ooohhhh!" Emma clapped her hands together. "A surprise? What is it?"

Mrs. Kim smiled. "You'll see."

I wondered what kind of surprise I could help with. I started to get a little nervous. What if she wanted me to sing or dance or something like that?

Before I could ask, Mrs. Kim had something to say to me.

"Devin, it was nice to hear from your mother," she said. "It was really sweet of her to be so concerned about Emma."

"Yeah, it was," Emma echoed.

"I told her we've been trying to get those memes taken down," Mrs. Kim continued, "but unfortunately, we haven't had any luck so far."

I looked at Emma. "I'm so sorry."

Emma shrugged. "It's, like, almost impossible to get them down once they're up."

"I know," Mrs. Kim agreed. "We reported them to the social media sites, but we haven't gotten a response so far. Still, you both did the right thing by telling us about it. Devin, your mom gave me the idea to call the school, to see what we can do to make sure nobody is harassing Emma about this on school grounds."

"Thanks," Emma said. "It hasn't been *so* bad, really."

Mrs. Kim sighed. "I feel bad for you kids," she said. "Devin, when your mother and I were growing up, it was a different world. There was no Internet, or social media, or memes, or any of this stuff. If something happened, no one was around to take a picture of it and post it publicly."

We drove up the palm-tree-lined driveway that led to Emma's house. The house was so big that I guess it was technically a mansion. It had a deluxe, in-ground pool and a lavish movie room.

"Why don't you and Devin go up to your room?" Mrs. Kim suggested to Emma. "I'll bring a snack up, and I'll let you know when your surprise is here."

"Great, Mom. Thanks!" Emma gave her mom a hug and bounded up the stairs, with me following close behind. I was getting to know my way around Emma's large house, but I still didn't want to take any chances of becoming lost in it.

Emma's room was like the rest of her house: really fancy. It was the size of about three of my bedrooms and had a bed, a sofa, a television, and this cool hanging chair dangling from the ceiling. Emma also has a huge fish tank mounted on the wall, with lots of brightly colored fish swimming around. It was like being at the aquarium. And there were tons of Brady McCoy posters hanging all over the room. He was Emma's favorite singer.

I noticed something different from the last time I'd been here. Emma had a beautiful new bedspread. It had a black-and-white pattern on it, with vivid blue, green, and pink stripes running through it.

"I love your new comforter!" I told her.

"Thanks!" She smiled. "I had to get a new one, because my mom got me a new mattress. I wasn't sleeping very well after those memes came out, so she ordered this fancy one from Sweden. It was bigger than my old mattress, so I got a whole new bed and blankets and everything."

"It's really pretty," I said. "Did the mattress work? Are you sleeping better?"

Emma shrugged. "A little. I told my mom not to bother, but she insisted. I would have preferred the invisibility cloak!"

We laughed as Emma's mom came into the room carrying a tray.

"Organic cherry juice mixed with sparkling water," she told us as she laid the tray on the table in front of the sofa, "and some blueberry, pistachio, and dark chocolate bark. They are all foods that help reduce stress and fuel the body. I got them to keep our Emma going during this rough time."

She bustled out, and Emma looked at me, her cheeks a little pink. "My mom can go totally overboard sometimes," she said, looking embarrassed.

"Don't worry. Remember that time when my family tried to get a wave started at one of our games? And nobody else would do it, so it was just the three of them going up and down, up and down? That was so humiliating!" I told her.

We munched on the bark (which was totes delish!) and drank our cherry spritzers while we chatted. I wanted to work my way up to Goalie-Palooza.

"Did it feel weird not being in front of the goal?" I asked her, trying to find out how she was feeling about the situation.

Emma put down her glass of cherry juice and frowned. "It did and it didn't," she explained. "At first it was so weird. I kept feeling like I was in the wrong place, like I was out of bounds. Then as the game went on, I got used to it. I had the other defenders with me, backing me up if I let one of the offense get past. I didn't feel so alone, like I can in front of the goal."

"What about you?" Emma asked. "How did you like being goalie?"

"It was intense," I admitted. "To be a goalie you've got to be part psychic and part gymnast. I never knew how tough it really is, Emma. But you're a natural. You can't give it up."

Emma opened her mouth, ready to tell me something, and I sat there eagerly waiting to hear what she had to say. Did Emma want to give up the goal for good? Or was she ready to get back into it?

Before she could speak, her mother's voice carried up the stairs.

"Your surprise is here, Emma!" Mrs. Kim's voice rang out. "You and Devin should come out to the back lawn."

Emma and I looked at each other, our eyes wide.

"Do you have any idea what it could be?" I asked her.

Emma shook her head. "Nada. Let's go find out!"

She grabbed my hand, and together we raced down the stairs and through her maze of a house to her backyard.

There was a large, grassy area near the in-ground pool. Emma's mother was standing there, talking to a young man dressed in yellow athletic shorts and a black T-shirt. He had light-brown skin, and when we bounded out onto the lawn, he turned and smiled at us, showing his dimples and bright white teeth.

"Girls, this is Danilo. Danilo, this is my daughter Emma and her friend Devin," Mrs. Kim said, introducing us. "Danilo is a private soccer trainer. He's here to help Emma build her confidence and to get her feeling comfortable in front of the goal again."

Danilo clapped his hands together and gave a little jump, his brown eyes sparkling.

"You're going to get right back into that goal zone, Emma, and you're going to feel great about it. Do you know how I know that?" Danilo asked her, rocking back and forth on his feet the entire time he talked. He wasn't much taller than Emma, yet his energy level seemed sky-high.

Emma looked at me, not knowing what to say. Instead she giggled.

"Because when I look into your eyes, I can tell. You've got the fire. You belong in front of that goal. You've got a wall up right now. But I'm going to tear it down!" he said. "Are you ready to tear that wall down, Emma? Devin, are you ready to help her?"

"Yes!" we both shouted, and then we looked at each other and started laughing.

"He's cute," Emma whispered to me. "And funny."

"Laughter is okay." Danilo smiled at us. "We're going to work hard, but we're going to have fun."

Luckily I was wearing sneakers. Emma quickly changed into her new cleats, and we got started.

"You know how you are going to get back into that goal zone, Emma?" Danilo asked.

"Um, kicking and screaming?" Emma said, half-joking.

"Emma! That's not the positive attitude I want to see from you!" Danilo said.

"I was just kidding," Emma said quickly. "I really don't know how I'm going to get back into the goal zone. Last time I played goalie, it was a disaster."

"Don't look back, Emma. You're not going that way." Danilo was full of motivational sayings. "We're only going forward. Right, Devin?"

"Right!" I yelled back. Danilo's enthusiasm was contagious. I couldn't help myself. "Onward and upward!"

"I like your attitude," Danilo said, smiling at me. Then he looked at Emma. "How you're going to get comfortable is by repetition. You're going to be getting your hands on that ball over and over again. When I'm done, you're going to be able to catch a ball in your sleep!"

"All right, now. Devin is the one who plays soccer in her dreams, not me," Emma protested.

"That's going to change, Emma," Danilo promised. "We're going to start soft. Easy catches, back and forth. Stand about twenty feet apart."

Emma and I faced each other on the lawn and tossed the ball, pretty softly at first, but then Danilo wanted us to throw harder.

"Now I'm going to kick the ball to you. Try to catch it," he said as he darted around the lawn, kicking the ball at both of us from different angles.

Emma dove one way, but the ball was aimed another.

"When you can't change the direction of the wind, adjust your sails!" Danilo called at her as he continued to race around.

Next he had us lie down on the ground, like we were about to do a sit-up. Danilo first tossed the ball above Emma's head, and Emma had to sit up to catch the ball before lying back down. Then he did the same to me. It was like a crunch combined with a passing exercise.

"Even if I never step foot in front of a goal again, I'll

have a nice six-pack after this workout," Emma joked. At least I hoped she was joking. The Kicks needed her in front of the goal!

Danilo had us do a few more warm-ups before launching into drills. If we'd thought he was high energy before, now he really kicked it up a notch!

"Sprint to the center! Now back up; the ball is coming. Catch it! Now to the right! The left!" Soon we were zipping around the lawn as quickly as Danilo was. We caught ball after ball. Danilo was right. I could probably catch one in my sleep after all of that.

"Slide to the right. Now the left!" He had us working on slide saves, high-diving saves, and backswings. We were doing every goalie move in the book.

Whenever we would make a mistake, Danilo would shout out one of his peppy sayings.

"If plan A doesn't work, stay cool. The alphabet has twenty-five more letters."

"I love mistakes. Mistakes are proof that you are trying!"

"Hard work beats talent when talent doesn't work hard."

He ended with, "It never gets easier. You just get better!"

Emma and I sat slumped on the grass, panting. Danilo was tough, but he'd made it so much fun. Mrs. Kim came out with some water bottles for us.

Emma looked relaxed and happy. Maybe this was the breakthrough she needed. I hoped.

"So, Emma, are you ready to take back that goal?" Danilo asked, still bouncing on his feet.

"I don't know," Emma admitted, and for the first time that day, I saw the smile fade from Danilo's face. "This training was a blast and I learned so much. But the thought of standing in front of the goal again makes me so nervous."

"Emma, you've got genuine talent as a goalie. I can see it, and I'm not just saying that," Danilo said seriously. "Your future is created by what you do today, not tomorrow. Don't worry about the last game, or the next one. Be the best you can be right now. The future will take care of itself."

"I know, but . . ." Emma trailed off.

"Maybe you just need a little more time before you step in for a game," I suggested. It seemed the perfect moment to bring up my idea to get Emma back into the zone. "There's this event that's just for goalies. It's called Goalie-Palooza, and goalies compete in different activities. It's really fun, with food and music. I think it could be just what you need, Emma."

"A goalie competition? I don't know," Emma sounded reluctant.

But Danilo was enthused.

"It's a great event! I've competed in it," he said. "You should definitely give it a try, Emma. Life is like a mirror. If you smile at it, it will smile back. This is your chance to shine."

"What a fantastic opportunity. Devin, do you have the sign-up information?" Mrs. Kim asked.

"I can email it to Emma," I said. My friend didn't look too happy about my idea. I started to feel a little guilty.

"Thanks, Devin!" Mrs. Kim beamed, but Emma just looked down at the grass.

"I'm not sure, Mom," Emma said softly.

"Emma, honey, you can do it. I know you can," Mrs. Kim said kindly.

Emma sighed. Whether she liked it or not, it looked like Emma was Goalie-Palooza bound.

CHAPTER Nine

"So I had to hula hoop while drinking this sports drink," Frida was telling us. We were sitting in the stands at our school's soccer field the following afternoon, watching the boys' soccer team play a home game against the Panthers.

"Could you do it? I can't hula hoop at all, never mind trying to drink something too." Zoe shook her head. "I'd end up covered in it."

"I learned for the commercial. I had never tried it before," Frida confided. "But Miriam told me that if a casting agent ever asks me if I can do something, I should always answer yes."

Frida was another example of how life was different in California. When I'd lived in Connecticut, I hadn't known anybody who was a TV star. Frida had had a big role in the TV movie *Mall Mania* with teen pop star Brady McCoy. She'd also gotten a lot of commercials since then too. She had made friends with an older woman named Miriam Hall, who used to be a movie star many years ago. Frida idolized her, and Miriam gave Frida lots of acting tips whenever Frida visited the senior home, which was about once a week.

Emma's eyes grew wide. "But what if you couldn't do it?"

Frida shrugged. "Fake it till you make it," she said, before chuckling in a deep, rich tone that sounded a lot like Miriam's. "But I did learn. I spent the entire weekend practicing, and boy, were my abs sore!"

"Mine are too after our training session with Danilo yesterday," Emma said. "How about yours, Devin?"

"I felt it when I got out of bed this morning," I admitted. "It was a good feeling. Danilo is awesome. I would train with him every day!"

Jessi pouted. "I wish I could have been there."

Emma slung her arm around Jessi's shoulder. "Sorry. I didn't know. It was a surprise. My mom said that next time you could all come. And," she added with a sly smile at Jessi, "Danilo is really cute. Almost as cute as Sebastian."

Jessi smiled back. "I'll believe that when I see it."

"Yeah, but Sebastian's only your friend, right?" Zoe asked teasingly.

Jessi shrugged. "What's wrong with being friends?"

Suddenly the crowd erupted into cheers, and we turned our attention back to the game.

José, a midfielder, had intercepted a pass from the other team and sent it to Steven, who was a striker, like me. Steven ran fast to keep up with the ball, and when he was on it, he kept it close. The defenders swarmed him, and I saw him looking around for a passing opportunity. Cody was open, and Steven had a clear shot. He passed Cody the ball. Cody got it and charged toward the goal. He kicked the ball, hard and fast, into the right corner of the net. The goalie missed it. Score!

The crowd went wild. Jessi jumped to her feet, clapping and cheering. "Way to go, Cody!" she yelled. Then she looked out over the stands. A lot of kids from school went to the games, and some other players on the Kicks were in the stands too. When we didn't have practice or a game of our own, we tried to support the boys' team, just like they did for us.

Suddenly Jessi dug into my side with her elbow and pointed to the right of us. "Who's that?" she asked.

A girl with long red hair had stood up, cheering along with everyone else. She held a sign that said in big letters: GO, CODY! She had drawn stars and soccer balls all over the poster too. There was even a pink heart in the bottom corner.

"I think that's Ciara," I said. " I'm pretty sure she's in my World Civ class."

"Hmmmmmmm," Jessi said as she slid back down onto the bench.

Emma, Zoe, and Frida looked at the girl with the sign and then back at Jessi. Then they looked at me, their eyebrows raised.

I threw my hands up into the air in bewilderment. I didn't know what was going on, or how Jessi was feeling.

The game continued, and we sat down. I could practically feel Jessi thinking next to me. Her entire body was rigid, and her brow was creased.

I tried a gentle approach. "I know you and Cody are just friends," I said, "but it still must be weird to see another girl here cheering for him."

"Yeah. Like, who is she?" Jessi wondered. "I never heard Cody mention her before."

"Maybe they've got some classes together," I suggested.

"Maybe," Jessi said. "But the sign? With a heart? That's more than just classes together."

"Wait. I'm confused. I thought you liked Sebastian now," Zoe said.

"I do. I mean, not like that." I gave her a look. "Okay, maybe like that." If Zoe was confused, Jessi sounded even more so. "But it feels weird to see this Ciara girl with a sign for Cody. He's been totally annoying me, and I thought I was kind of over hanging out with him. Now I don't know." Jessi let out a big sigh.

"No matter how smart you are, matters of the heart will always make you dumb," Frida interjected. "At least that's what Miriam always says."

"That makes sense, because I am feeling pretty stupid right now," Jessi admitted. "Like, why am I feeling this way?"

"Because it's totally confusing," I shared. "Steven texted

me the other day and asked if we were just friends. What am I supposed to say to that? I'm not allowed to date, and even if I were, I don't think I'd be ready. It's just way too complicated. But at the same time I really like hanging out with Steven."

Emma smiled sympathetically. "I'm so glad that the only crush I have is on Brady McCoy. It makes life so much easier."

Zoe put her arms around Emma and Frida, who sat on either side of her.

"We've got each other, and that's what counts," she said. "No matter what!"

That broke the tension, and we all relaxed as the game heated up and took back all of our attention.

The Panthers tightened their defense after Cody's goal. The game was at a stalemate until Steven squeezed through their defense. He had a clear path to the goal, when a Panthers' defender came barreling toward him. It looked like he was trying to trip Steven. Yet Steven outmaneuvered him, deftly guiding the ball away and giving himself a clear shot at the goal, which he took, and pulled off.

Steven had tied up the game 2–2, and the Kangaroos had control of the ball. Jake charged down the right side of the field, zooming past the Panthers' midfielder, and passed to José. José passed it to Cody, who pushed back the defenders and scored again.

The crowd cheered, and as we all clapped for the

Kangaroos, I saw Jessi watching Ciara out of the corner of her eye. She was waving her sign in the air with excitement, calling Cody's name. *This must be so weird for Jessi,* I thought. If it had been another girl holding a sign for Steven, I don't know what I'd have been thinking.

It was Kangaroos 3, Panthers 2, and time was running out on the clock. All the Kangaroos had to do was keep the Panthers from scoring, and so their defense tightened up like crazy. Another scoring opportunity appeared as the ball got passed from Kangaroo to Kangaroo down the field, before being passed to Steven. He dodged around a defender as he made his way for the goal. Right before he reached the penalty box, he kicked the ball, hard and high over the goalie's head.

Goal! The score was 4–2 and it stayed that way until time ran out on the clock.

"Their defense has really strengthened this season," Zoe remarked as people started leaving the stands.

I nodded. "Steven said Coach Valentine was working on improving their defense," I said. "It was their weak spot in the fall."

Emma shuddered. "Coach Valentine! I don't miss having him as a coach."

She was talking about the time when Coach Flores had been called away in the fall for a family emergency. The boys' season had been over, so Coach Valentine had stepped in to coach us. He was really tough, but I did learn a lot from him. And even he wasn't as tough as

Coach Darby, my soccer coach from the winter league. I definitely liked Coach Flores the best. She was so nice and made soccer fun.

"The boys certainly don't have it easy with him," I said. "But look how they've improved!"

As we walked onto the field, I saw Ciara talking with Cody. Jessi hung back, not sure what to do. When Ciara left the field, Cody and Steven came over to us.

"Great game, guys!" I said. "That was some awesome footwork out there, Steven. I don't know how you got that goal. I'm impressed."

Steven's cheeks got a little redder, and they'd already been flushed from the game.

"Thanks, Devin," he said.

Jessi was also congratulating Cody, but she wasn't her usual loud, energetic self.

"Hey, do you guys want to come out for pizza with us?" Cody asked. "The team is going out to celebrate."

Jessi shook her head right away. "Sorry, but I've got too much homework."

Steven looked at me hopefully. "Devin, can you come?"

"Let me text my mom," I replied. I was torn. Part of me hoped she would say no. It would be weird being there without Jessi.

But my mom said yes (why is it that parents are strict until you want them to be?), and soon I was at Vinnie's Pizza with the boys' soccer team. Luckily, some of the other Kicks were there, including Grace, so it didn't feel too strange. Ciara was there too, and I noticed she sat next to Cody.

Steven and I ate pizza and did a play-by-play analysis of the game.

"So when he went left, I went right," Steven said.

We had a good conversation about the game, but I couldn't help feeling like something—or actually, some-one—was missing. It was strange not having Jessi and Cody teasing each other and joking around as Steven and I talked. I wondered if Jessi and Cody would be able to keep hanging out with each other, now that this whole Ciara thing was making life more complicated.

If they didn't, could Steven and I still be friends?

CHAPTER TEN

The next day at school Emma told us all at lunch that there would be a twist to the training session we would be invited to.

"Danilo wants to train on the beach," she explained. "My mom will drive us all there on Saturday."

"That sounds fun, but Coach Flores always says she doesn't believe in beach training," Zoe pointed out. "She says it can build bad habits, since the grass field is so different."

Emma nodded. "I told Danilo that. He actually called Coach Flores, and she said it's okay to do it once in a while, especially since Danilo thinks it will help with my goalie fear."

"Goalie fear? That sounds like a contagious disease," Jessi joked.

"Well, it's a real thing," Emma told her. "And you want

me to get over it, right? So I'll get back in front of the goal?"

"Totally!" Jessi agreed.

"Well, I'm looking forward to it," I said. "I've lived in Southern California for months now, and I hardly ever go to the beach."

Zoe shook her head. "That's because you're always playing soccer."

"See? It's a perfect combination," Emma said. "Soccer *and* the beach!"

That night when I was video chatting with Kara, she couldn't believe I was going to be beach training on Saturday.

"There are three inches of snow on the ground here!" she complained. "It's spring break next week, and I still need to wear my winter coat and boots outside!"

I nodded. "I miss the snow. But not when it just keeps snowing, and snowing, all the way into spring."

Saturday came, and it was a beautiful day (like most days in Southern Cali), perfect for beach training. Normally we'd have a game on Saturday, but it was the start of spring break and no game was scheduled. Coach Flores had thought about canceling practices during break too, but we had convinced her to keep them. We had a game the following Saturday, and everybody wanted to be ready for it.

That morning I dressed in a T-shirt and shorts, following

Emma's instructions. I put on flip-flops, because Emma had said that we'd be training barefoot. After breakfast Emma's mom pulled up in her big van. Emma, Jessi, Zoe, and Frida were already inside, along with two of Emma's brothers, the youngest ones. Sam was eight, and Peter was ten. I took the last remaining seat, and Mrs. Kim drove off.

It was true that I hadn't spent much time on the beaches since I'd moved to California from Connecticut. I lived close enough, and lots of kids in my school loved to surf and boogie board on weekends. But Zoe was right—most of my free time was spent on soccer. So I was pretty happy to be able to combine both for Danilo's training session.

"I'm psyched for the beach training," Jessi remarked as we headed down the freeway.

"I've heard that practicing on sand is less stressful on your joints," I said. "And that can mean fewer injuries. That sounds good to me. It was no fun being benched at the start of the season, after I pulled that muscle."

"That's a good reason, but that's not why I'm psyched," Jessi said. "We're going to be training next to the big, beautiful, blue ocean!"

Frida gave a little shudder. "I am not a fan of sand. You can spend five minutes on the beach, and when you get home, you find it in your clothes, in your hair . . ."

"And even in your underwear!" Zoe finished, singing the words. Everyone laughed, except for Emma's two little brothers, who were absorbed with whatever game they were playing on their tablets in the backseat.

Soon we reached Blue Hollow, one of the beaches that is part of California's state park system. It's not the kind of beach with a boardwalk with games and ice cream stands. It's a beautiful stretch of sand on the border of the big, beautiful, blue ocean, as Jessi would say. On the other side of the beach is a white fence, and beyond that, private homes are nestled into small hills dotted with scraggly green plants.

Even though it was a sunny spring day, it was still sort of chilly for swimming. But several surfers in black wetsuits were lined up on the shore. Some people strolled along the water's edge, talking or walking dogs. Some beach chairs were scattered about, filled with people reading or relaxing.

Mrs. Kim parked, and we exited the van. Emma's brothers dumped their tablets and ran across the sand, screaming with happiness, and throwing a football back and forth. Danilo came running toward us, dressed in a white T-shirt and shorts, with a soccer ball under his arm.

"You're right," Jessi whispered to me. "He *is* cute."

"Good morning, Mrs. Kim!" Danilo said brightly. "Good morning, girls!"

"Good morning!" we all said back to him, rather loudly. Danilo had that effect on everyone, I guess. Instant energy.

"You know Devin, and this is Jessi, Frida, and Zoe," Emma said, pointing to each one of us.

"Thank you for doing this, Danilo," Mrs. Kim said. "Have fun training. I'll let you know when lunch is ready."

"Thanks, we will," Danilo said. Then he turned to us and clapped his hands. "Okay, girls! Let's warm up with a jog!"

He took off toward the water's edge, and we followed him. Danilo stayed on the sand, but as we jogged, the water would sometimes creep up and touch our bare feet. Emma squealed the first time it happened.

"It's so cold!" she said.

A light breeze was blowing, and it felt good. As we jogged, I felt a sort of Zen thing happening. I moved my feet to the rhythm of the waves. I watched the white gulls swoop and soar in the blue sky above. Every breath I took, I tasted salty air.

We circled back and headed up the beach to an area where Danilo had set up four cones. I wasn't winded from the jog at all. If anything, I was feeling even more energized.

"This is one of my favorite drills to do on sand," he said. He stood at the end of the line of cones. "What I'm going to ask you is to move sideways, weaving between the cones. When you get to the last cone, stop, and I'll gently toss the ball to you, and you'll gently kick it back to me—with the top of your foot, or your leg, since you're not wearing any shoes. Got it?"

We all nodded.

"Great!" Danilo said. "Everybody line up behind the first cone. After you kick it back to me, move to the back of the line."

We lined up. I was first. I moved sideways, weaving between the cones like Danilo had showed us. It was way different from moving on grass. I felt more resistance in my calves.

When I got to the end, Danilo sent an easy lob at me. I bounced it back to him with my shin.

"Nice, Devin!" he said.

We did that drill for a while, so everyone got several turns. Then we stopped, and Danilo took two cones and placed them the same distance apart as the official goalposts in our middle school league—twenty-four feet.

Danilo stood between the goalposts.

"Devin, try to score," he said, throwing me the ball. "Emma, keep your eyes on me!"

I put down the ball and dribbled for a few steps, then faked left and kicked right toward the goal. Danilo made a flying dive into the sand and caught the ball, sending sand flying everywhere when he landed.

"Nice try, Devin!" he said. "This is one of the reasons I wanted to practice on the beach. It can be intimidating for a goalie to take a nosedive into hard earth and grass. But diving into sand is a piece of cake."

"Plus, no shoes to fly off," Emma quipped.

"Come on, Emma," Danilo said. "The goal is yours. Your friends will try to score. Don't let them."

Emma nodded. "Okay. Here goes." She took her place in front of the goal. "Bring it on!" she said bravely. "Give me your best shot!"

Danilo tossed the ball to Jessi.

"Here it comes!" Jessi called out. She kicked one over Emma's head. Emma jumped up, caught it, and landed firmly on her two feet.

"Nice try!" Emma said. "All right, who's next?"

We took turns shooting at the goal, and pretty soon Emma was jumping around and rolling and diving into the sand.

"You're doing great, Emma!" Danilo cheered her on.

We all ended up taking turns at guarding the goal, and I had to admit, it was more fun than playing goal on the field. There wasn't that little voice in the back of my head wondering if I would get hurt if I dove for the ball.

After that, Danilo led us in a few more drills. The sun was high in the sky when we heard Mrs. Kim's voice.

"Lunchtime!"

Danilo nodded. "It's a good time to break."

A delicious smell hit my nose as we ran toward Mrs. Kim's setup. She was cooking hot dogs on a small charcoal grill. A pile of already-cooked dogs was sitting on a small table, along with a bowl of potato salad, a platter of dumplings, and a tray of cut-up mangoes and melons.

"Wow, Mom, this looks awesome!" Emma said, grabbing a hot dog. "I'm starving!"

"I thought we could make it a little party," her mom replied. "Before you go to Goalie-Palooza tomorrow."

Emma frowned. "Don't remind me! I'm so nervous, just thinking about it."

"You've got nothing to be nervous about, Emma," Danilo said. "You're a great goalie."

The rest of us agreed with Danilo. Jessi put an arm around Emma.

"Don't stress about it, Emma Emma Bo-Bemma," she said. "Today, we eat. Tomorrow, you rock Goalie-Palooza!"

Zoe held up her hot dog. "Cheers!" she said, and we each picked up a dog and tapped them together, just as if we were clinking glasses.

Then we each took a bite. Frida made a face.

"Frida, is something wrong with your hot dog?" Mrs. Kim asked.

"No, it's delicious," Frida replied. "It's just . . . it's got sand in it."

"Mine is fine," Zoe replied. "Maybe you're just a sand-attractor, Frida."

Frida squirmed. "I think you're right. It's in my under-wear, too. I can feel it."

Emma giggled. "Oh no, Frida!"

"See? If you get nervous tomorrow, just think of Frida with sand in her underwear," Jessi said.

Frida shook her head. "Please don't!"

"I hope you can all come to cheer on Emma," Mrs. Kim said.

"My dad already offered to drive," I told her. "I know Emma has to get there early, to register and warm up before the competitions."

"There's that word again. 'Competitions,'" Emma said, frowning.

"There *are* competitions, but Goalie-Palooza is mostly about having fun," Danilo said. "I have been going for the last ten years."

"Yeah, you mentioned that," Emma said. "You said you competed, right?"

Danilo grinned. "Speed champion in my age group, three years in a row. But I think you should enter the rapid-fire-defense competition, Emma."

Emma's eyes got wide. "That sounds intense."

"It is," Danilo said. "But I think you'll be great at it."

Emma took a deep breath and turned to her mom. "Thanks, Mom, for all of this. I'll make you proud."

"You already do," her mother replied.

"Awwwwwww!" Zoe and Frida said together.

"So, Emma, are you any closer to becoming the Kicks' goalie again?" I asked.

"Weeeeeellll . . ." Emma dragged out the word. "Maybe. Let's see what happens tomorrow."

I crossed my fingers behind my back for luck. The Kicks needed Emma back on goal.

I just had to wait one more day to see if my Goalie-Palooza idea would save the day—or make Emma quit being a goalie for good!

CHAPTER ELEVEN

The next day Dad and I picked up Zoe and Frida. Then we went to Jessi's house to get her. We found her outside—talking to Sebastian!

Jessi nodded at us when the van pulled up. Then she said something to Sebastian, and he hopped onto his bicycle and pedaled away.

I was in the front passenger seat. I turned around to Jessi as she got into the car, and raised my eyebrows.

"What?" Jessi asked innocently. "He just came by to say hi."

"I like his bicycle," Zoe said.

"I think Jessi likes more than his bicycle," Frida said.

"Oh boy. Girl gossip," my dad said. "Just what I need on a Sunday morning."

"We'll save it for Goalie-Palooza," I promised my dad, giving Zoe and Frida a warning look.

Zoe got the hint and quickly changed the subject. "So, what exactly is going to happen when we get there?"

I turned to the festival's page on my phone and started to scroll through the info. "Well, there are supposed to be food stands, and booths with soccer stuff to buy," I replied. "And then there are competitions held all afternoon for different age groups. Some of the competitions are for skills like speed and keeping the ball in the air. Then there's the one Emma's doing, the rapid-fire challenge. It says here that goalies have to defend ten balls in thirty seconds."

"Whoa. Do you think Emma can handle it?" Jessi asked.

I nodded. "If Danilo thinks so, then I believe him. She'll do great."

Dad drove us to the county fairgrounds, where the festival was being held. The parking lot was packed, and as we got out of the van and walked toward the festival, we saw throngs of people walking around, most of them in soccer uniforms and goalie gear.

"I've never seen so many goalies in one place!" Zoe exclaimed. "There are tiny goalies." She pointed to a group of goalies who looked about as old as my sister, Maisie.

"And giant goalies." She pointed to some really tall college guys.

Dad turned to me. "Is it okay if I meet up with you during Emma's competition? I'd like to look around, and I don't want to cramp your style."

"Sure, Dad," I replied, and before he could ask, I said, "My cell phone is charged."

"Great!" Dad said, and then he took off. He loved soccer even more than I did, so I knew he'd find a lot to do.

"Let's try to find Emma," Zoe suggested, and we headed down a row of booths.

We hadn't gone far when Jessi stopped. She pointed to one of the booths. "That is too funny!"

The stall was selling T-shirts with goalie sayings on it. EAT, SLEEP, SAVE. One with a heart that read, I'M A KEEPER! KEEP CALM AND LET THE GOALIE DO THE REST. And my favorite, FEAR THE KEEPER.

"These are great," I agreed.

Frida had wandered down a little farther. "You won't believe this. They have goalie food, too!"

"Goalie food?" I wondered.

But Frida was right. There was an Italian food stand that sold goalie cannolis. We used to get cannolis in Connecticut. They were a type of Italian pastry—a tube of crispy fried dough with a sweet cream filling.

I read the rest of the menu. "Goalie stromboli. Goalie ravioli. Chicken salad with goalie aioli."

I shook my head. I'd known that Goalie-Palooza would be about goalies, but I hadn't known it would be this intense!

Zoe dragged me to another stand, laughing. "Check this out," she said. "Goalie guacamole!"

"That actually looks awesome," I said, and then I ordered some with a side of chips. Between the four of us, it was gone in seconds.

"That tasted like regular guacamole to me," Zoe said. "I

mean, what makes it goalie guacamole?"

"Goalie guacamole, goalie guacamole," Jessi repeated in a singsong voice. "I don't know, but it's fun to say!"

"Maybe we should find the competition area," Zoe suggested. "I don't want to miss Emma."

"Good idea," I agreed, and we made our way through the crowd.

At the end of the row of booths we found a schedule of events attached to a post in the ground. It was a pretty complicated chart, so Zoe squeezed in past the other people looking at it to get a closer look.

"Girls twelve to thirteen, rapid-fire defense, field C, at twelve thirty," Zoe reported when she came back to us. "That's coming up soon. We should find field C."

Thankfully there were big signs by each of the competition areas, and we found field C pretty easily. It was also easy to spot because Emma's entire family was there, sitting in a row of chairs set up on the sidelines. My dad was talking with Mr. Kim, and he waved when he saw me.

We walked up to Emma's mom. "Hi, Mrs. Kim!" I greeted her.

"Girls! Good to see you," she said. "Emma will be competing soon."

She pointed to a row of girls lined up on the other side of the field. I recognized the uniforms of some of the teams in our league. The goalie from the Roses was there, and also the Panthers. Emma stood out in her blue Kicks uniform, and because she was a head taller than everyone else. She was third in line.

A young woman in green shorts and a white shirt jogged out onto the field in front of the spectators.

"Shhhhhh! It's starting!" Mrs. Kim hissed.

"Welcome to our rapid-fire-defense trial," she told the crowd. "My name is Jenna Rogers, and I'll be running the trial today, along with my teammates." She pointed to a line of women who all looked to be about her age.

"We'll be shooting ten rapid-fire balls at each contestant," she continued. "The goalie with the most saves wins."

Five shooters lined up in front of the goal, and the first goalie took her place. A ref on the side of the goal blew a whistle, and the first shooter sent a ball hurtling toward the goal.

The goalie stopped it with a kick. Then another ball came speeding to her, and she ran to catch it but missed. Three, four, five, six, seven . . . the balls kept coming. After the last ball, the ref blew his whistle.

"Seven!" he called out, and everyone clapped.

"Man, that looks tough," Zoe said.

The next goalie went up, and she made six saves. Then it was Emma's turn. She looked nervous, but her face relaxed when she saw all of us with her family.

"Go, Emma! You got this! We love you!" Zoe shouted, and we all cheered.

Emma nodded, and then she got a look of focus on her

face like I'd never seen before. The referee's whistle blew.

Bam! The first soccer ball flew toward Emma, and she caught it and threw it back.

Bam! The next one skidded toward her, and she kicked it back.

She caught the third and fourth. She kicked the fifth. The sixth ball flew over her head, and the seventh whizzed past her before she could get it.

"You can do it, Emma!" Jessi cheered.

Emma caught the eighth ball. And the ninth. She was all the way on the right side of the goal when the last ball came flying at her, all the way to the left.

Emma dove. Her long arms were outstretched before her, and her long legs stretched out behind her. She grabbed the ball inches above the ground and then landed, facedown. She jumped to her feet as the whistle blew.

"Eight!" the referee yelled.

We started clapping and cheering like crazy, but we quieted down when it was the next player's turn. I glanced over at Frida and saw her typing on her phone.

"Were you on your phone the whole time?" I asked.

"I got a great shot of Emma," she replied. "So I made a new meme."

"Frida!" I cried. "Why would you do that?"

She grinned. "Check it out."

She handed me the phone. Zoe and Jessi peered over my shoulder. It was a photo of Emma flying through the air after the ball. Frida had added the words "I believe . . . she can fly."

"That is perfect!" Zoe cried.

Frida took back the phone. "I'm uploading it to Quik-Pik. I've got seventeen thousand followers there, ever since I did *Mall Mania*."

Frida tapped her screen, and we turned back to the competition. Most of the girls got six or seven saves. But two got nine saves, tying for second place, and one girl even saved them *all!*

When the competition was over, the ref handed out ribbons. Emma came running up to us with a yellow ribbon that read, Rapid-Fire Defense, 12–13, Third Place.

"Third place!" Mrs. Kim gave Emma a hug. "I'm so proud of you."

"You did great!" I said.

"You sure did," Frida said. "Everyone thinks so."

"Everyone?" Emma asked.

Frida held up her phone. "Look."

Emma turned pale. "Oh no."

But she took the phone from Frida and looked at it. Her eyes got wide.

"This is . . . awesome!" she said "I mean, it's a lot better than the last meme. I still don't know how I feel about being famous, though."

"Well, get used to it, because you've got more than a thousand likes so far," Frida said proudly. "Maybe we can never get rid of the old meme, but from now on maybe people will know you as the goalie who can fly."

Emma's eyes started to tear up. "You guys! I guess I've got to stick to being a goalie now, right?"

"Of course you do!" I said. My plan had worked.

"I think this calls for some goalie cannoli," Jessi said.

"Goalie cannoli? What's that?" Emma asked.

"You'll see," Jessie promised, with a mysterious smile, and we all headed back to the stalls. We ate goalie cannolis, and fried goalie raviolis, and Emma bought a FEAR THE KEEPER shirt. Then we joined an impromptu soccer game on one of the empty fields, just for fun. No uniforms, no cleats, just kicking a ball around.

It was about then that I realized that my whole weekend had been one big Soccer-Palooza, and I couldn't have been happier!

CHAPTER TWELVE

I woke up on Monday morning with a big smile on my face. It was spring break week, so that meant sleeping in without an alarm. Emma was going to be on goal again. Life was looking pretty good.

The smell of bacon lured me out of bed and downstairs.

"Mmmmmm, bacon!" I said as I stepped into the kitchen, rubbing the sleep out of my eyes. Since my mom was into healthful food, bacon was saved for holidays and vacation. And when we did have it, she got it from a meat vendor at the farmers' market, and it was all humanely raised, antibiotic free, and a bunch of other stuff I didn't really understand. All I cared about was that it was delicious.

Our kitchen was open to our living room, and I could see Maisie sitting on the sofa, a plate on her lap piled sky-high with bacon. We weren't usually allowed to eat in the living room either, but she was munching as she watched cartoons.

"Wow!" I said to Mom. "What's the occasion?"

Mom smiled. "I thought you both deserved a spring break treat to start your week," she said. "You've been doing so well in school and working so hard at soccer, this is a little reward."

"I've been doing well in school and at soccer too!" Maisie called out, her mouth full of bacon. Maisie had joined her elementary school soccer team last fall. My dad was the coach. Sometimes some of my friends and I helped out at their practices.

"You both have!" Mom said. "And this is why you're getting a special breakfast and are allowed to eat it in the living room. Devin, help yourself to eggs and bacon. I've got to get started on work."

My mom worked from home. She was a small-business accountant, and she'd gotten a lot of new clients in the last few months.

"Thanks!" I said as she poured herself a cup of coffee and headed into her office, which was right off the kitchen.

I piled my plate high with breakfast and plopped down onto the couch next to Maisie.

"Don't even think about changing the channel," Maisie said to me without taking her eyes off the television.

I rolled my eyes. "Don't worry about it," I said. Instead I grabbed my phone and checked to see if there were any messages.

I had two texts. The first one was from Steven.

Are we still on for the zoo today?

Ugh! I had totally forgotten. Before all the Jessi-Cody drama had started, the four of us had made plans to go to the Pinewood Zoo the first day of spring break. It was a small one, with a petting zoo and a merry-go-round. There was also a really nice lake there with picnic benches all around it and concessions stands nearby. We were going to have lunch after seeing all the animals.

The second text was from Jessi.

I totally forgot about the zoo 2day. What do you want to do?

The sounds from Maisie's cartoons blared around me. I brought my plate of food into the kitchen so that I could eat in peace.

I munched on some bacon before I texted Jessi: I'll go if you want to.

After all, Jessi kept saying she was still friends with Cody, right? So if that was true, why couldn't we go to the zoo with the boys today?

OK, Jessi texted back. My mom said she would drive. Pick you up at 12?

OK, I answered, before replying to Steven: Yep! We'll be there around 12:30.

Cool, he answered, with a smiley face.

I really hoped that Jessi and Cody would be cool and that we would all get along and have a fun day!

We met at the front gates, underneath a sign that said PINEWOOD ZOO AND PARK. There were large, wood paintings of some of the animals at the zoo, with a cutout where the animal's face would be. You could stick your own face in it and take a picture.

Jessi and I were horsing around, taking photos of each other, when Cody and Steven walked up.

Now, if this had been like the days before Jessi had become friends with Sebastian, Cody would have run over and started joking around with us. But he seemed a little nervous as he strode toward us, no smile on his face.

"Jessi, can we talk?" he said.

Jessi had her head sticking out of the body of a penguin. "Um, okay, give me a second," she said as she came out from behind it.

Steven looked at me and smiled. "Hey, Devin," he said.

"Hey," I smiled back, eager to tell him all about Goalie-Palooza, but it looked like Cody was going to say what was on his mind.

"I guess, I'm just . . . wondering why you've been hanging out with Sebastian," Cody told her.

Jessi shrugged. "He's nice. We're just friends. Why, does it bother you?"

Cody's face grew flushed. "It does, and you know why, Jessi. Don't make me say it."

"Say what?" Jessi asked.

Cody shook his head in exasperation. "That I like you, *like you like you*. You know what I mean. And I thought you *liked me liked me* too."

"I did. I do. I . . . I don't know!" Jessi cried out, frustrated. "Maybe this wasn't a good idea."

She turned to me. "Devin, let's go to the petting zoo," she said, and then she grabbed me by the arm and started dragging me away.

I glanced over my shoulder and gave Steven an apologetic look as Jessi hauled me off. Once we'd paid the admission and gotten through the gate, Jessi kept pulling me, past the owls and hawks and other large birds kept in large outdoor cages. We followed the winding path until we were at the petting zoo. A bunch of goats and sheep were behind a wooden fence. A woman sat at a table, selling plastic cups of food to feed the animals with.

Jessi pulled out two dollars from the pocket of her jeans and got two cups, one for me and one for her. She glanced over her shoulder.

"Good, they didn't follow us," she said, speaking for the first time since she'd had it out with Cody.

She went up to the fence, and a large goat immediately put its front legs on the top post and began ramming its head into Jessi's hand.

Jessi laughed as she scooped out some of the food and put it into the palm of her hand. The goat began to eat hungrily.

"Don't be greedy!" she chided the goat.

I spotted a little one in the corner and I called to it, trying to lure it over. It came over hesitantly, obviously nervous about maybe having to battle it out for the food with the bigger goats. I squatted down by the first slat of the fence, where there was room for the little goat to stick its head through. I placed some of the food on the palm of my hand, and it began gobbling it up, getting slobber all over my hand.

"Ewwwwww!" I said, holding up my messy palm to show Jessi.

"Don't worry, Devin," she called as she continued to feed the big goat, "they've got a hand-washing station."

I gave Jessi the rest of my food and then washed my hands really well in the outdoor sink. Then I spoke up.

"So, I feel bad leaving Steven back there," I said.

"I know. I'm sorry," Jessi said. "I just can't deal with Cody right now. And I need some Devin time. Are you with me?"

I nodded, and then I quickly texted Steven. **Sorry. We'll catch up to you later.**

K, he texted back, and I hoped he wasn't upset.

"Come on, Devin." Jessi was pulling me once again. "Let's go to the reptile house."

I shook my head. "I'm not a fan of snakes."

But in we went, and Jessi kept pointing out how cool the turtles, lizards, and snakes were. I shivered. They gave me the creeps, but Jessi seemed fascinated by everything we saw. I got the feeling she was avoiding talking about what had happened with Cody, but I didn't push her. I was just really glad when we got back outside!

We looked at the prairie dogs (which were really cute), and the next section in the zoo held some larger animals, like camels, alpacas, and ostriches. A lot of families were there, moms and dads pushing strollers, kids oohing and aahing over the animals. It was really adorable, but I was starting to get hungry.

"Let's go eat," I said, and this time I pulled Jessi away from the penguin display and walked her over to the lake, where the concessions stands were.

We both got plates of chicken fingers and french fries, and cups filled with lemonade, and brought them to a table overlooking the lake. A pair of swans was swimming in it. The whole scene was very peaceful and tranquil.

I dipped a chicken finger into some honey mustard and looked at my friend, who seemed fascinated by her french fries. She wouldn't make eye contact with me.

I put down the chicken finger.

"Okay, we need to talk about what happened," I told Jessi, who was dipping a french fry into ketchup.

Jessi groaned and put the french fry down on her plate, without taking a bite.

"I know," she said with a sigh, and then she put her head in her hands.

"I know it was really awkward back there," I told her. "But you can't just run away from Cody. You guys need to figure this out."

"It's just so confusing," Jessi shared. "I did have a crush on Cody. Now I kind of have one on Sebastian. But even if I were allowed to have a boyfriend, I'm not sure if I want one right now."

I nodded. "That's exactly how I feel. I have a crush on Steven, but right now I'd rather focus on soccer, schoolwork, and my friends."

"It's just too complicated," Jessi said. "I want to hang out with my friends too, and not worry about all this stuff. So what do I do now?"

"Maybe it doesn't have to be complicated," I said. "Let's hang out with our friends and have a good time. Why worry about all this other stuff? We should all be able to be friends. There's plenty of time for everything else later."

"Yeah, but Cody obviously isn't comfortable with that," Jessi said.

I shrugged. "Too bad for him then. It's his decision if he wants to stay friends or not, Jessi. If he doesn't, then that's on him."

Jessi smiled. "You're right, Devin. I'm not going to worry about it anymore."

We ate, between bites talking and joking. I felt a lot

better, and I could tell that Jessi did too.

So when Cody and Steven entered the picnic area and came over to our table, we were both in a better frame of mind to deal with the situation.

"I, um, I want you to know something, Jessi," Cody said, sitting down next to her. "I wish you liked me the way I like you. But if not, I guess it's cool if we're still friends."

"I'm glad you said that," Jessi said. "Honestly, Cody, I'm not sure how I feel. So if we can be friends until I figure that out, that would be awesome."

"Sure," Cody said, nodding. "So when you're done eating, friend, do you want to check out the reptile house?"

"We already went," I replied. Then I shuddered. "Too many snakes!"

"Then let's check out the otters," Steven suggested.

"Yay!" Jessi cheered. "Otters are so cute!"

"Much cuter than snakes," I agreed.

"I just need to finish my fries, though," Jessi said.

With a grin, Cody scooped up some fries from her plate and popped them into his mouth.

"French fry thief!" Jessi yelled.

Cody scooped up the rest and took off running. Jessi ran after him. I cleaned up our trash and Steven and I took off after Cody and Jessi.

"You'll never see this french fry alive again!" Cody was saying, and Jessi was laughing was she chased him.

Steven and I looked at each other and smiled.

"I'm glad things are back to normal," he said.

"Me too!" I told him.

The Kicks had a game against the Adams Atoms on Saturday. Emma would be back in front of the goal. Now that things were looking settled between Cody and Jessi, I was hoping all the Kicks would be in the zone for the game—the winning zone!

CHAPTER THIRTEEN

"Hey, it's the girl who can fly!"

We'd had a few Kicks practices over the break, and now it was Saturday and the Kicks were warming up on the field of the Adams Atoms. The game was about to start, and spectators were wandering onto the visitors' side of the field. People were pointing at Emma, but this time nobody was laughing. Instead they were cheering her on.

"Awesome dive!"

"You fly like a superhero!"

Emma was next to me as we did stretches and crunches on the field, and I knew the pink in her cheeks was from blushing and not from exertion.

"Frida's meme really blew up," I remarked.

Emma nodded. "It's practically wiped out the memory of the old one."

"You're welcome!" Frida called out, a few players down from us.

"Thank you, Frida!" Emma called back. "You're *my* superhero."

Coach Flores clapped her hands. "Okay, girls! Let's get into the zone. We're on the field soon."

We all moved to the sidelines, and I saw Emma start to put on her goalie gear.

"Emma's back on goal, everybody!" I announced to the team.

Everyone cheered, and Zarine walked up and hugged her. "I'll be able to play again next week," she said. "I'm glad you're back on goal. We need you there."

"You have got to come to Goalie-Palooza with me next year," Emma told her. "It's so much fun, and there are so many goalies there."

Zarine smiled. "I won't miss it!"

Emma nodded. "Definitely!"

Coach Flores clapped again. "All right, girls, here's our starting lineup."

She put Emma on goal. Anjali, Frida, and Giselle were on defense. Grace and Taylor were in the midfield. And Megan, Jessi, and I were strikers.

We took our places on the field. The Atoms wore bright red-and-yellow uniforms. My stomach did a little flip. We had played them in the fall during the regular season, and lost.

Megan took her place for the kickoff in the center of the field, against a tall, blond Atom. The ref blew the whistle, and the Atom got the ball. Jessi zipped over and kicked it away from her before she could get more than ten feet.

Megan and I flew down the field after Jessi. The Atoms defense was right on us. It seemed like there were six of them, but there were only three! Wherever we moved, somebody was blocking us. Jessi tried to pass to me, but one of the Atoms intercepted it and charged toward the Kicks goal.

She made it past our midfielders. Then Anjali ran up to challenge her, but this Atom had some fancy footwork. She kept turning her back on Anjali, dribbling the ball in circles. Then she quickly darted left and tore past Anjali, speeding to the goal. Halfway there she sent the ball flying.

Emma jumped up to catch it. The ball slipped through her fingers and bounced into the goal. She face-planted into the dirt.

Uh-oh, I thought. *Will she be okay? Will she give up?*

But Emma just jumped up and brushed the dirt off her shorts. She threw the ball back in and planted her hands on her knees, looking forward with determination on her face.

That's my Emma! I thought proudly. We were one goal down. But that didn't mean we were out.

Megan, Jessi, and I worked hard to get past the Atoms

defense. We quickly figured out that if we kept passing, they couldn't keep up with us. We got within goal range. I took a shot that the goalie blocked. The next time we got back there, Jessi took a shot, but didn't score.

She walked back to me, shaking her head. "I bet their goalie went to Goalie-Palooza too," she said.

The Atoms regained control of the ball and took it down to Emma again. A chest-height ball came screaming at her, but she bounced it away with her body. Then a huge grin came across her face.

"That's right, superhero!" I yelled.

Maybe it was seeing Emma flawlessly block that goal, but new energy surged through me. Grace passed the ball to Megan. She passed it to Jessi, who passed it back to her. Then Megan passed it to me.

I barreled past the defenders and took a shot as soon as I got into goal range. It was a long, smooth, high shot that soared over the goalie's head and into the net, nearly grazing the top bar. The ref blew his whistle.

We had scored! The game was tied 1–1, but right after that the ref called halftime.

As I jogged back to the sidelines, I glanced at the visitors' bleachers. Mom and Dad were there with Maisie. Emma's whole family was there, and I saw Jessi's mom too. Sebastian was in the stands with his sci-fi friend Isaac. And then I spotted Steven and Cody with some of the guys on the Kangaroos. Cody was holding a sign that read GO, KICKS!

I nudged Jessi and pointed. "I know," she said. "Pretty cute, right?"

Coach Flores launched into a pep talk and praised us for getting past the Atoms defense.

"Let's try a new lineup for the next half," she said. "Hailey, Zoe, and Brianna, you're strikers. Anna and Olivia, you're in the midfield. Sarah, Jade, and Gabriela, I want you on defense."

"Emma, are you okay to stay on goal?" Coach asked.

Emma nodded. "No problem!" she said confidently.

Sitting out wasn't my favorite thing, but I knew that Hailey, Zoe, and Brianna would do great. And sometimes it was fun to sit on the bench, because you got to watch the game. Jessi, Frida, and I sat together. We cheered on our team and especially our friends Zoe and Emma.

Having Zoe on offense was a smart move. She was small and zipped around like lightning, and the Atoms defense did not know what to do with her. She scored in the first few minutes of the half.

"Go, Zoe!" we yelled.

The score was Kicks 2, Atoms 1. But the Atoms recovered quickly. One of their players sent a long, high pass flying down the field. It was a pretty bold thing to do, but the tall Atoms striker was right on it and got control of the ball really quickly. Then she sent a ball zooming past Emma, and the score was tied 2–2.

By this time the Atoms had figured out that they should put all their defense on Zoe. Which might have sounded like a smart idea, except that they underestimated Hailey and Brianna. Olivia got the ball to Brianna, who had a clear shot to the goal. She took it, but the Atoms goalie blocked it.

Still, the Atoms focused their defense on Zoe. Hailey got control of the ball, and she and Brianna passed it downfield. Brianna took a low, speedy shot at the goal. The unprepared goalie didn't get to it in time. We were up by one point again!

There was less than a minute left in the game. I looked at Emma. Her eyes were laser-focused on the field. The Atoms took the ball toward the goal. The tall blond girl got control of the ball again. She took a shot from the very left side of the goal zone, sent it toward the goal at a weird angle.

The ball was about three feet to Emma's right. She jumped. She stretched out her arms, just like she had done at Goalie-Palooza.

She caught the ball.

"Eeeeeemmmmmaaaaaaa!" I was beside myself. I was screaming and jumping up and down.

The game ended thirty seconds later. The Kicks had won, 3–2! All of us on the bench rushed onto the field to hug our teammates. Then we lined up to shake hands with the Atoms.

When we got back to the sidelines, a bunch of people were there to congratulate the team. Steven and Cody and some of their friends, including Ciara. And also Sebastian and Isaac.

Grace, my co-captain, stood on the bench. "Great game, everybody! I call pizza celebration!"

Everyone cheered—the Kicks and our fans—and some started heading toward the parking lot. Jessi looked at Cody and his friends, and Sebastian and Isaac. She walked up to them.

"You guys want to come for pizza?" she asked.

Cody raised an eyebrow. Sebastian looked confused.

"'You guys' meaning . . . ," Sebastian began.

"Everybody," Jessi said, looking at him, and then at Cody.

Cody nodded, and Steven smiled at me, and then everyone was talking and heading off the field. It was all good.

Emma was comfortable being back in the goal zone. Jessi was back in the no-drama zone. And me . . . I was glad that our team was in the victory zone. The Kicks record was now 3–1.

The state championships were in our sights!